# ASHES

## *In*

# YOUR MOUTH

### A HOUSE OF AUSHER NOVEL

# EMBER DRAKE

# ASHES
## *In*
# YOUR MOUTH

# Content/Trigger Warning

Warnings for Ashes in Your Mouth contain intense and potentially upsetting themes, including:

- ❖ Violent sexual assault
- ❖ Kidnapping
- ❖ Violence and gore
- ❖ Mental health issues/grief management
- ❖ Addictions
- ❖ Explicit sexual content

# CHAPTER 1

Roland was on Kezia like a man starved for contact. The moment their lips touched, he had pulled her naked body against his bare chest. His hands slid along her throat and then back up her neck, entwining his fingers in her curls as he deepened their kiss. He held her face in one hand for a moment, then slipped it down along her body, exploring her like it was his first time. As if he did not believe she was real.

He left her gasping for breath when he pulled his mouth away to kiss along her throat. He lingered at her neck as his hands continued to explore every inch of her bare flesh within his reach. When he felt her reach down to undo his trousers, he quickly got up to remove them. He took a moment to admire her in her nudity. She was glorious, with her light brown skin and soft gray eyes. The steady rise and fall of her breasts combined with the dark look in her eyes made his cock twitch with greater need.

He loomed over her, his hands shaking as he pushed her legs apart.

"Touch me more," she said in a breathy tone. "Please."

As he knelt between her legs, he looked at her breasts again. They were perfectly round, soft mounds of flesh that were just the right fit for his hands. Not too big, not too petite. Her nipples were a few shades darker than her skin, and they stood erect and wanting. He palmed them lovingly before his mouth was on her, and he murmured sweet nothings of how perfect and beautiful she was into her skin. And that she was his.

He repeated his words over and over into her skin like a mantra. The warmth of her small hands was on him, moving over his shoulders and down his back. Lightly clawing at him. As he lay on top of her, his weight pressing her down into the bed, she moaned her approval. She traced the lines of his muscles as his tongue lashed at her tender nipple, and her thighs parted more for him. He eagerly settled between them, rubbing himself against her, his erection heavy and full of desire.

He lifted his head and inhaled sharply, swearing under his breath. She was so hot and wet for him he almost came with the contact. He had to be inside of her, but he knew he would not last if he entered her now, and he wanted to enjoy the feeling of her beneath him. And he wanted her to know how much he loved and missed her.

Roland kissed his way down her chest, to the flat of her stomach, until he reached his destination. He inhaled her scent deeply and made a half groan, half growl. She smelled like fresh spice on a crisp fall day. It was intoxicating. He whisked the dark, curly hairs that covered the dark, delicate flesh of her sex with the back of his fingers, making her shiver. With two fingers, he explored the swollen outer curves of her lips. She was wet and blossoming in front of him. Her hips moved in a small, but noticeable roll as he spread her with the tips of his fingers. He found the narrow slit that made his cock ache.

He was so entranced by the sight of her, and had her hand not urged him against her, he would have been content to stay like that. Leaning forward, he kissed her inner thigh, then slowly pushed a finger into her. A sharp gasp escaped her lips before turning into a moan.

He went in as deep as he could, feeling her clamp down around him as he slid through the wetness of her sensitive, swollen flesh. With agonizing slowness, he withdrew his hand, then reentered her with two fingers. She was tight and his hands were large. He could feel he was stretching her out as he palmed her. His fingers were as deep inside her as they could go, so he put his mouth on her, opening her up with his tongue. He caressed her, tasted the silky honey his fingers worked to produce, and continued to push them slowly in and out of her, with the occasional twist.

She moaned his name as her fingers pulled his hair. His tongue and fingers worked inside her until he felt the muscles of her thighs tense up. She cried out with her release. It was a pleasing cry of need and painful longing as she came into his hand and on his tongue. She writhed in his mouth, soaking his fingers as she pulled them deeper within her core as she came undone.

He licked and stroked her as he rode out the climax with her, working her into another. When he felt she had

3

enough and her head fell back, he removed his hand with the care of a gentle lover. All of his fingers were soaked with her juices, and he licked them clean of the evidence of her desire before he stood back up.

Again, he admired her for a moment, looking down at the mess he made of her. He placed his hand around his cock and stroked it while she watched through hooded eyes. By no means was he done with her. He grabbed her by her hips and turned her onto her stomach. Something he had not done in sixteen years. He pulled her to the edge of the bed, lifting her hips to tuck a pillow beneath her. He rubbed the smooth expanse of her ass with one hand as he guided the head of his cock to her swollen slit. She was still dripping like a sieve, and he could feel the hot steam from where his fingers played just moments before. Once more, he groaned as he pushed inside of her.

His member was thicker than his combined fingers and she was still so tight, so he had to move into her a little at a time. He would push into her, then withdraw to just his head. With each slow thrust, he made her take a bit more of him.

This time, she swore aloud as her fists knotted themselves in the bedding.

He smiled wickedly as he continued to work his way into her, inch by glorious inch. "Yes, love. Take all of me," he purred, ramming the rest of his cock into her.

Bracing herself, she pushed back against him, forcing him deeper into her. He leaned forward over her until his mouth was at the nape of her neck. Burying himself in her completely, he bit down on her without breaking skin. She gasped as her head fell back and she groaned. He felt her body shake as she reached her climax again, and he came growling behind her.

He filled her with his seed until he had no more to give, then pulled out of her with a wet smack. Once again, he had made a mess of her, and she looked well satisfied and spent. So was he. She had pulled quite a lot of his energy out of him. In more ways than one.

The warm glow of the will-o-wisps flitting about the room beautifully silhouetted her form as she lay half-conscious on the end of the bed. He picked her up and laid her down properly, then lay down beside her. She immediately curled into him and fell asleep, and he followed suit. It had been far too long since he felt that good.

The sounds of soft moaning woke him up, but they were not ones of pleasure. His love was crying in her sleep.

"Kezia," he whispered. "Wake up, love, you're having a bad dream."

He squeezed her lightly against him, stroking her arm until her lashes fluttered and her eyes opened. She looked up at him and breathed a sigh of relief.

He frowned down at her. "What's wrong?"

"Nothing. It was just a dream, and I barely recall it now," she replied, smiling wryly at him.

He knew she was not being honest with him. They had spent days locked in their bedroom since she woke up, and every night she had a nightmare. He knew it was to be expected, considering how long she was in a coma, but he would help her in any way he could. Even if it meant staying up all night to tire her out enough to even fall asleep. She did not like or want to sleep on her own and he would not leave her.

5

"Well, I'm here to listen if you remember it," he murmured, kissing her on the forehead. "Try to get back to sleep."

"I don't want to sleep. I've slept enough for a lifetime," she argued.

"Then what would you like to do? It's too early for anyone other than Nox to be awake," he told her. "If you're hungry, I can make you something."

She shook her head. "Just lay with me."

"Of course. You're sure nothing is bothering you?"

She took a few moments to think on his question, then she sighed.

"What is it, my love?"

"I could feel and hear everything that happened in this room while I slept," she admitted. "I could feel how sad you and our son were with my condition. I could feel our daughter's fear before my father took her body. I couldn't shut it out."

Again, he frowned when she cried.

"Our son was neglected because of me," she sobbed.

He shushed her, squeezing her against him as she cried into his chest. "That wasn't your fault. None of it was," he assured her.

"No," she said through gritted teeth, pounding on his chest. "It's yours. You should have felt her. You should have looked for her."

"Had I better understood our bond, I could have found our daughter in time and brought her home. But I was so lost in my sadness that I didn't find her or care for our son."

"Why didn't you look for her?" she cried, fighting to get out of his hold and failing. "How could you not know?"

She continued to cry and howl in anguish, her eyes flashing red as she fought against him. Roland could feel Rhydian's distress over his mother. He knew she could feel it, too.

"It's all right, love. I will fix this," he said as he placed his hand on her head. A warm blue light emanated from it, and he shushed her again when she panicked. "It's all right, love. Just rest for now. I'll be here when you wake up."

She fought against him until she stilled into sleep. He knew she would be angry with him when she woke up, but he had work to do. They had already pushed back Rhianwen's memorial services when Kezia woke up. After finding out that his brother had killed her and took over her body, the family was beside themselves with grief. He would make things right again. Though their family would never be whole, what was left would be together.

# CHAPTER 2

T he air was thick with the scent of popcorn and the sound of laughter as the group of shapeshifting clowns left the arena. It was time for the main event, and as the spotlight centered on them, the crowd hushed in anticipation. Raesh took his place at one end of the arena, and Sacha stood at the other, her bare feet firmly planted on the ground. With a nod from Raesh, the act began.

Raesh's hands moved with lightning speed as he sent knives whizzing through the air. He aimed each blade with precision, slicing through the space around Sacha. With every throw, Sacha's powers came to life. She raised walls of earth to catch the knives, then let them crumble back into the ground. The audience gasped as the knives seemed to dance all around her as she moved around the arena, yet not once did they touch her. It was a deadly ballet of earth and blades.

Raesh took a deep breath and launched himself into the air. In a display of fire and blood, four feathered wings appeared out of his back, shimmering like a magpie's feathers, spread wide for all to see. He soared above the arena, his silhouette cutting through the dim light. The collective inhale of the audience urged him on. With a swift motion, he drew his knives, their blades catching the torchlight as they spun through the air.

In perfect harmony with him, Sacha summoned pillars made of stone from the ground. The pillars rose and fell in a choreographed dance, creating a dynamic and ever-changing landscape. His knives flew with deadly accuracy, each one aimed to miss Sacha by mere inches. The audience watched in awe as Sacha moved gracefully among the pillars, her movements fluid and precise as she caught and discarded each knife thrown at her.

Raesh, high above the arena, prepared to throw his final knife. Sacha, with her back to him, raised a massive wall of stone behind her. With a powerful flap of his wings, he hurled the knife with all his strength. The blade sliced through the air and headed straight for Sacha.

In a fraction of a second, Sacha created a dais of earth beneath her and the wall and spun it around to face him. Her hands glowed with elemental energy as she caught the knife between her palms, the force of the throw causing her to take a step back. The audience sucked in a collective breath, then erupted into thunderous applause as Sacha held up the knife casually, a broad smile on her face.

Raesh descended gracefully, landing beside her. They took their bows, the crowd's cheers ringing in their ears.

As they left the arena, they could not help but smile at one another. Their stunts were growing more and more elaborate as time went on. Sacha was getting older and more powerful, but it would soon be time for her to retire. Though he continued to smile down at her, the thought made him sad. He would miss her, and he did not look forward to having to train her replacement.

Once they were clear of the arena, Sacha left Raesh's side to go clean herself up and rest a bit. Aiden appeared shortly after, sneaking up from behind him, as always.

"Looking good out there!" he cheered, clapping. "I was actually worried she wouldn't catch that last one."

"I do not understand why. We have practiced that routine countless times," Raesh replied. Although he would never admit it, he was a little worried himself.

"I'm not looking forward to her retirement party. You two work so well together."

Raesh frowned at that. "She is still in good shape and strong. It will be some time before she retires."

"Still, I think you should tone down your stunts a little. I don't want to see her get hurt."

Raesh nodded in agreement. "What did you want to see me about?" he inquired, wanting to change the conversation. He did not like feeling sad. It made him uncomfortable.

"Right! I wanted to discuss our finances with you."

"Yes, what of it?"

"Walk with me, Andy," he started, moving to exit the tent.

Raesh followed suit. Something was wrong now. Aiden never brought up money around him, and he was rarely ever serious.

Aiden stopped briefly for Raesh to catch up. "Patronage is at an all-time high right now." He continued to walk. "Especially with you and Sacha's performances. People love the danger and excitement."

"But..." Raesh trailed off.

"But the upkeep of the tents and equipment, as well as our homes, is expensive."

"All right."

"And the upkeep of your lover is eating into the savings now," he admitted. "He reads and shops an awful lot."

"Ah, I see. And what do you propose I do about it?"

"Do you love him, Raesh?" he asked, stopping to face him.

Raesh's eyes went wide in surprise for a moment. Aiden had never called him by his chosen name before. "Why do you ask?"

"I ask because when you're not rehearsing or performing, you're with him. Provided we're close to the club."

"You can take more of my pay for his continued care and expenses," Raesh offered. "I do not require much to live on."

Aiden sighed. "That's not the point, old boy."

"Then what is?"

"You clearly love the man, though you seem reluctant to admit it. I want to see you happy, Andy. I'm sure he does, too."

Raesh sighed with exasperation. "What are you getting at?"

"You have his contract. Why not take him out of that overpriced brothel and bring him home?"

Raesh stared at Aiden blankly. "No. He is happy where he is, and safe. I cannot ask that of him."

"He doesn't know who you were, does he?" Aiden asked with a concerned tone.

"He does, and he is fine with it," he replied.

"If you're worried about the Emori, we have security for that."

"I said no," he replied with a practiced, calm demeanor. "He is my mate. I wish to keep him safe and happy. He would just get bored traveling with us, anyway."

"Are you sure about that?"

"Yes. Now, if that is all, I wish to go check on Sacha."

Again, Aiden sighed. "Very well. Off with you then. I have a show to get back to, anyway."

Raesh inclined his head to Aiden before stalking off to Sacha's trailer. When he arrived, she was already sound asleep on her cot. As he turned to leave, she moaned softly and turned, facing him. He noticed bandages on her hands. He frowned as he left, making sure to close the door quietly. They would discuss it later, but he was going to rework their stunts for her safety.

# CHAPTER 3

*I* *mprisoned in the deepest part of the underworld for the last fifty years was Vitani's soul. She had been a powerful witch in her mortal life, but her many wicked deeds and transgressions against her village had gotten her drowned. Even dead, she had proven to be formidable. Her soul had to be chained down.*

*Ozmir had received reports of living mortals tampering with the veil between realms and a rebellion among the imprisoned souls. He split his pack of Anabi into two groups: one headed by their leader, Azier, and the other led by Azier's mate, SeVhon. Ozmir went with SeVhon to investigate the rebellion.*

*"I wager Vitani started this one," SeVhon laughed.*

*"I'd be a fool to bet against that," Ozmir replied.*

*The moment they arrived at the prison, the heated air from an explosion of power blew them both off their feet. The force of the blast sent them careening into a nearby stone wall, the impact of their bodies creating a sizable crater before they bounced off and hit the ground. As they recovered from the shock of the explosion, staggering to their feet, Ozmir heard the distinct sound of large bits of metal clinking to the ground as several chains broke, followed by a noise that sounded like fabric being torn. It was the veil being ripped open. When he looked up, he saw a grinning Vitani slip through the tear with other damned souls.*

*Ozmir swore aloud. He commanded the Anabi to stop the rest of the souls from escaping while he and SeVhon went after those that got through the rift. With his hands holding the sides of the rift and a chanted spell, he closed the tear behind them as other souls tried to force their way through. As the tear sealed up, a net formed within the opening to hold back the escaping souls. They looked like fish wriggling and writhing as they tried to get through. Once the tear was closed, the arms and legs of the damned souls that got through instantly became translucent wisps of ethereal smoke that dissipated in seconds. Ozmir knew Vitani's presence in the mortal world would only bring chaos and destruction.*

*On the mortal side of the rift, Ozmir and SeVhon encountered a fierce battle between Azier and his Anabi with a group of witches, their powers crackling in the air like an electric storm. The Anabi must have moved through the earth using their elemental powers for faster travel. Although Azier's pack had cut down several of the* witches, *their efforts were hampered by the shadow wraiths—spectral beings bound by dark magic to the witches' cause. These wraiths, ephemeral and malevolent, darted through the fray, sowing confusion and striking with relentless precision.*

*Ozmir wasted no time. His eyes burned with intense focus, and with a sharp inhale, he summoned his inner fire. The air around him shimmered as he gathered his power, a halo of heat waves distorting the carnage before him. Then, in a blinding flash of white light, Ozmir unleashed his fury. A wave of searing-hot flames burst forth from his fists with a dramatic gesture as he punched the very fabric of the air in front of him. The inferno surged forward, engulfing the shadow wraiths in an all-consuming blaze. Their shrieks of despair echoed briefly before silence fell, the darkness they embodied vanishing into the ether.*

*The remaining witches, realizing the tide of the battle had turned, abandoned their fight. With hurried chants and desperate movements, they fled into the shadows, leaving behind the smoldering remnants of their fallen allies. Azier's Anabi, now unimpeded, wasted no time in pursuing their original mission. Capturing the escaped souls that lingered beyond the rift. Azier and SeVhon stayed behind with Ozmir, awaiting further orders.*

*"They won't be able to handle Vitani," Ozmir spoke. "Transform. I need you two to track her."*

*The mated pair nodded before shifting into their bestial forms. SeVhon was a sleek black wolf with bits of colored moss embedded in her fur, and eyes that shone like the moon. In that form, she was swift and silent, a master of earth and shadows. Azier, a massive white wolf with green vines trailing along his body, was a force of raw power and strength. The trio set out to track down the malevolent soul.*

*Vitani's trail led them through dark forests and into a desolate wasteland. Her dark magic left a path of corruption and decay that made it easier for SeVhon and Azier to track her. Finally, they reached a ruined temple where Vitani's soul had taken refuge. A thick, malevolent energy hung in the air; the ground was scorched and barren. It reeked of death and black magic. Ozmir could feel the wicked soul's presence, a dark and twisted force that threatened to consume everything in its path. The feel of it made his skin tingle and crawl.*

*When they went inside, the melodic hum of an ancient chant vibrated through the chamber, deep and primal. It started with a low, almost guttural vibration, as though the earth itself was exhaling a sound older than memory. The notes intermingle, each one sliding smoothly into the next, forming an unbroken wave of sound that seemed to ripple through the air. Some voices grounded the chant in a steady, rhythmic pulse, while others rose and fell in haunting overtones—like whispers of wind threading through ancient trees—layering the hum. As they rounded the corner, they saw a group of witches hovering around a long stone altar where a dark-haired girl with equally dark skin had been bound and gagged. She writhed and screamed around a gag as they performed a forbidden ritual with Vitani's soul floating above her.*

*Before they could stop what Ozmir recognized as a ritual to bind a soul to a new vessel, a witch had plunged a blade into the girl's chest. SeVhon growled and darted forward, her movements a blur as she dodged bolts of dark magic. Azier charged in, breaking through the ranks of witches, rending fabric and flesh. But by the time they got*

16

through the mob, it was already too late. The girl was dead, they could see her soul, and Vitani's was gone.

Slowly, the girl's body rose, her eyes glowing a vibrant white. She pulled the dagger out of her chest as if it were a mere splinter and tossed it aside, then she took her hand and placed it on the still-bleeding wound. With a faint glow of her magic, the wound healed, only leaving the blood stain behind. Azier and SeVhon returned to Ozmir's side. The remaining witches stood guard as others dressed the girl's body in dark red robes and gave her a book.

"What are your orders, Lord Ozmir?" asked Azier.

Ozmir sighed. Gods could not interfere in mortal lives, and Vitani had a new body to live with, but she was far too dangerous to allow to roam free. "Capture her," he said after a few moments.

Vitani smiled wickedly. "You can try, dragon."

Ozmir growled, his hands lit with white fire as he charged forward with SeVhon and Azier at his sides. Vitani laughed and created a vortex of dark magic. Azier and SeVhon took on the remaining witches that aided Vitani while Ozmir faced the evil witch alone.

Vitani and Ozmir clashed with a deafening force of power. The battle was fierce. Vitani's magic was powerful, but Ozmir noticed she clung tightly to the book given to her. It was an old grimoire. He could feel the power emanating from it. Separating her from it was something he knew he needed to do.

He called his familiars to help him. SeVhon's speed and agility allowed her to strike Vitani's weak points, while Azier's strength kept the wicked soul at bay. Ozmir channeled his divine energy, casting powerful spells that weakened Vitani's defenses.

*In a final, desperate move, Vitani unleashed a torrent of dark energy, but Ozmir stood firm. With another blinding white light, Ozmir was able to snatch the grimoire from her. Ozmir held the book in one hand and grabbed Vitani by the throat with the other. He passed the cursed tome off to SeVhon for safekeeping.*

*"Release me at once," Vitani screamed, as she struggled in Ozmir's hold.*

*He ignored her cries and chanted an incantation that summoned the full power of the underworld to bind Vitani in chains of divine light. The chains bound her soul, and Vitani screamed in fury and despair as she was dragged back to the underworld; her power broken, her spirit subdued.*

*After Vitani's soul had been extracted, the body he held disintegrated into black dust. Ozmir knew that the underworld's defenses needed to be fortified to prevent any future breaches. Vitani would also need to be moved to a more secure prison with no chance of contact with the mortal realm again.*

*Once more, he sighed. Mortals were becoming more and more corrupt. He was starting to see why Zaven despised them so. He would talk to his twin about what occurred that night to see about binding the darker souls before sending them down to him. For now, he would seal Vitani's grimoire away to prevent anyone from finding it and releasing her again. His mother would surely be proud of his work.*

Dorjan grimaced at the memory. Though soon, he would have his revenge against his mother and brother. His mother for how poorly she treated him, despite his obvious admiration and devotion to her and his work. His brother for his neglect and utter indifference to how he and their mother treated him. Worse, his brother's abandonment left him to be subjected to more of their siblings' torment and their mother's cruelty. For his brother was the golden prince in her eyes and he was the poor copy, unworthy of the love she showered upon his brother, who had no time or interest in it. Dorjan was the dutiful, obedient son. So, why was he the one that was banished?

Dorjan snorted with laughter at how ridiculous his thoughts were about his family, but he would see them pay for their transgressions. He looked down at the husk of the woman he had taken to his bed that evening. He was still getting used to being in Rhianwen's body. It was not going well at all. Even when he shapeshifted to his own body, he still could not contain the lustful urges he felt so strongly. Since Kezia's awakening, it had only gotten worse. He wished she and his brother would find something else to occupy their time together.

# CHAPTER 4

Sixteen years. She had missed sixteen years of her life. Of her son's life. His first words, first steps, birthdays, scraped knees, and bedtime stories—all gone in the blink of an eye. So many moments she could never get back.

The door creaked open, and Roland walked in. He had kept her distracted for the first few days since she had been awake, but he still had a business to run, and Luxor could only do so much on his own. And then there was his job as the shepherd of drowned souls. So, she had been left alone with her thoughts and painful memories of what happened to her, though it was only for a few hours.

Roland had a wry smile on his scruffy face as he walked over to her. "You're awake. How are you feeling?" he asked, sitting beside her.

"As well as I can be, all things considered," she replied.

He frowned at that. "I brought something for you."

"I'm in no mood for gifts."

"You'll like this one," he promised as he signaled someone at the door.

In popped Lynnox, rolling in a chair with wheels. "Mornin' ma'am! So glad to have ya back," she beamed.

"A wheelchair?" Kezia asked.

"Yes, I thought you might want to get out of bed and move around," he said. "Just until you can walk on your own again."

"Roland, we're on the third floor," she said, bewildered.

He chuckled. "Don't worry, love. I took care of that as well."

"All right," she sighed.

Roland carefully lifted her out of the bed and placed her in the chair. "So, where would you like to go first?"

"I'd like to see my son, please."

"He and Dorian went into London while ya were sleepin', but he should be back soon," Lynnox replied.

It was her turn to frown. "Then I would like to go outside and get some sun."

"All right, how about going to the garden?"

She nodded, and he rolled her out of their room with Lynnox behind them. When they reached the stairs, she saw flat boards aligned going down. Gingerly, Roland wheeled her down the make-shift ramp.

On their way out, they ran into Ariel. When Kezia looked up at him, she noticed that his dark hair was turning gray, and his face was showing signs of aging, but he was still strikingly handsome.

"Ariel!" she squealed, perking up at seeing her old friend.

"My queen," he smiled, bowing his head. "Glad to see you up and about. How are you?"

"Happy to be awake. What have you been up to?"

"Not much lately. Just helping around the estate and keeping everyone safe."

"Ariel has expanded his pack, and they've been handling security for us," Roland chimed in.

"That's wonderful! Have you found a mate yet?" she asked, narrowing her eyes at him.

Ariel froze, his eyes wide. "Uh…"

"Kezia," Roland sighed.

"You're not getting any younger. You should've found someone by now," she said with the sternness of a loving, but worried, mother.

He laughed with mild discomfort. "I just haven't had the time, and I'm barely over a hundred. I still have time."

"No, you don't," she fussed.

"All right, all right. Enough of that, love. Ariel has work to do, so let him get back to it. You can bark at him later," Roland laughed.

Kezia pouted. "Fine, carry on."

Ariel bowed his head again, then mouthed 'thank you' to Roland.

"I saw that," she growled.

Roland and Ariel laughed as they waved goodbye.

"C'mon, let's get you outside. The fresh air and sun will make you feel better," Roland said as he wheeled her out the back entrance that led to the garden.

As soon as they were outside, she closed her eyes and raised her head up. The sun was warm and felt good on her face. She took in a deep breath, then let it out. And then, like a torrent, the tears came. She broke down into heavy sobs, and Roland came from behind her to kneel in front of her.

He had a worried look in his whiskey brown eyes. "What's the matter, love?"

She was crying so hard that she could not answer him. So, he held her until she could, making soothing noises as he rubbed her back.

"It's going to be all right, I promise. It's just going to take some time, is all."

"I want to see my son, but I'm such a mess right now. No wonder he hasn't been to see me," she admitted.

"He's tried to, but I wanted you to myself for a bit. I'm sorry for that."

She gave him a sympathetic look, remembering he felt her loss the hardest. And now she was crying over a son she did not know, ignoring her husband's feelings in the process. The tears came rushing down again, and all she could do was apologize for not considering how he was feeling.

"It's all right," he said. "I understand. You're his mother. There's no need to apologize for wanting to see him more than me. I've had you longer than he has," he smiled.

She looked at him. "And you will always have me," she sniffled. "I wouldn't even know what to say to him."

"Then let him talk," he suggested. "He's shy, but I'm sure he has a lot to tell you. He always snuck into the room to talk to you. You just have to listen."

She nodded, choking down another sob.

"That's my girl," he smiled. "Now, shall we walk around for a bit? I have a specialist coming to see you later to help get you back on your feet."

Again, she nodded, not trusting herself to speak without crying.

While strolling around the garden, Roland filled her in on what she missed out on. He told her how Rhydian behaved as a child, that he was a stubborn, but intelligent little devil. She could tell it was hard for him going through his memories with her about their son, but he continued anyway. He had spent little time with Rhydian as he got older, but he still watched him from afar. Even he had difficulties when talking with the boy, especially with Rhydian's emotions all over the place. Roland still was not good with his own feelings.

That afternoon, the specialist Roland hired arrived to help her with her rehabilitation. After waking up from her coma, her body was frail and her muscles had atrophied from years of inactivity. Though feeding on Roland's energy had lessened the damage over the years, she still had a ways to go for recovery. The specialist devised a comprehensive plan to help her regain her strength and mobility.

Kezia began with gentle exercises to rebuild her muscle strength and improve her coordination. Initially, she struggled with simple tasks like standing and walking, but with the support of her husband and the specialist, she gradually progressed to more complex movements. They celebrated every small milestone, like her first steps or lifting a light weight, each victory sweeter than the last.

# CHAPTER 5

Despite her physical triumphs, the emotional toll of missing sixteen years of her life weighed heavily on Kezia. Her initial progress was slow. Her muscles were weak, and she experienced frequent fatigue. There were days when she struggled to complete even the simplest exercises, which led to frustration and moments of doubt. She also faced occasional pain and discomfort as her body adjusted to the increased activity.

She still grappled with feelings of guilt for not being there for Rhydian, and anxiety about her ability to connect with him. Nightmares about the birth and her time in the coma would often disrupt her sleep, which made it harder for her to stay motivated during the day.

Roland tried herbal remedies to help with her mood, but nothing had seemed to work. Soon, she did not want him around outside of feedings, and she declined to see Rhydian just yet. She was not ready for it. Roland was at a loss about what he should do next.

He floated in the grotto as he thought, the trio of mermaids swimming in circles around him. After a few hours of him ignoring them, Ianthe and Nerissa swam off. Most likely to create mischief or drown someone and eat them, he thought. He really did not want to have to deal with one of their victims' souls later. Maraja was always the one to stay behind with him.

The redhead poked her head out of the water between his legs and eyed him carefully. "You seem lost today. I thought you'd be happier now that your wife has returned to you."

"I am," he sighed. "But she's having a rough go of it."

"Oh," she replied as she rested her arms on his stomach, followed by her head. "What do you intend to do about it?"

"I honestly don't know," he admitted.

"Have none of your herbal remedies worked for her?"

"No, but her body's doing fine. Mostly. It's her mind that still worries me."

"Oh." She paused for a moment. "Are there no spells or other magical solutions?"

"I can't trust those methods. I don't want any lasting negative effects on her mind or body," he explained.

"What if I had something that could help her? What would you give me for it?"

"Something like what?" he asked suspiciously. The mermaids were never keen to help Kezia with anything, especially Maraja. She hated Kezia the most.

"If I offer you my tears, would that please you?"

Roland's eyes widened in surprised realization. "Maraja, I could kiss you!" he exclaimed, standing up.

"I would like that very much," she grinned.

He grabbed her face and kissed her, and without a word, he leapt out of the water. He sprinted towards the house, his feet pounding against the wet stones. Inside, he fumbled for an empty bottle, his mind racing. His pulse quickened, but not from exertion. He was excited to have a solution to his dilemma. Returning to the grotto, he found the three mermaids waiting, their glistening tails catching the faint luminescence of the underwater cavern. Maraja had explained to the others what he had wanted and why. The other two, Nerissa and Ianthe, exchanged glances, their eyes narrowing with a mix of curiosity and jealousy. They could not hide their disappointment— pouting like children denied a treat—over the kiss he had shared with Maraja. Each one took their turn adding their tears to the bottle. When the bottle was full, he sealed it carefully.

"Thank you, girls. You don't know how much this means to me," he smiled.

"Can we get kisses, too?" asked Nerissa.

"Yes, please!" Ianthe chimed.

"Of course, anything for my girls." He gave them both kisses, then made the trek back to the house.

Once back inside, he went into the kitchen, surprising the staff, to get to work making a tincture of the mermaid tears. He infused it with his own power to strengthen it. Roland grumbled and cursed at himself for not thinking of using mermaid tears sooner, but his mind was elsewhere. He knew this would only be a temporary solution to

Kezia's mood, but it would give them the time they needed for her to feel better on her own.

After he bottled the infused tears, he went up to see Kezia. She was sleeping peacefully for once, and he did not want to disturb her just yet. He padded softly into the in-suite bathroom and got a hot bath started for her. She always enjoyed those, especially after her rehab.

He sprinkled healing herbs into the bath, then went back into the room to get her, leaving the tincture on the table next to the large quartz crystal tub. When he walked back into the room, she was sitting up, scowling at him.

He smiled nervously. "Sorry if I woke you."

"Why are you here? I'm not hungry," she said in a tired voice.

He frowned at her tone. "I know, but I wanted to give you something."

"Don't you have work to do in your office or a soul to console?"

Again, he frowned at her tone. He did not understand the anger she was feeling. "Please, love, I only want to help you," he pleaded.

Her expression softened after a moment. "I'm sorry. What did you have for me?" she asked, her hands folded neatly in her lap.

"Can you walk, or do I need to carry you?"

"I can walk, but I could use some assistance."

He quickly made his way over to her as she pulled her legs over the side of the bed.

"Where are we going?" She took hold of the arm he offered and stood up.

"Not far, just to the bathroom."

She gave him a quizzical look as she weakly took a few steps. He caught her when her legs went out from under her.

"Take your time, my love," he said, his tone gentle. "We'll get there."

She took a deep breath, then let it out before she tried again.

When they made it to the bathroom, he sat her on the plush bench. He slid off his trousers with deliberate care, the fabric whispering against his skin as he moved. Turning to her, his hands were gentle as he reached for the soft fabric of her nightgown, easing it up and over her shoulders with a touch that spoke of quiet reverence.

"What could you possibly have that's in the bath?" she inquired.

"You'll see," he grinned.

He wrapped his arms securely around her, lifting her with a tenderness that seemed to melt the air between them. Carefully, he stepped into the warm water, the steam curling upward in delicate tendrils, and lowered them both into its soothing embrace. The dried herbs perfumed the air around them. Once they were nestled together in the bath, the heat spreading like a balm over their skin; he leaned forward and reached for the tincture bottle resting on the edge. The glass felt cool against his fingertips as he brought it closer, the translucent blue liquid inside catching the soft glow of the candlelight.

She eyed the little clear bottle curiously when he handed it to her. "What is this?"

"Mermaid tears. The girls filled a bottle for me so I could make a tincture for you," he explained. "I infused it with my magic to strengthen it. It's to help with your melancholy."

She frowned at the bottle she was clutching. "Have I gotten so bad?" she whispered.

He longed to say 'yes,' but the thought felt too callous to voice. Yet dishonesty was no option either. Choosing his words with care, he said, "All of us just want to see you well again." His tone softened as he added, "Rhydian, especially—he's been so worried about you. He wants you to be a part of his life, love."

"And will this make me better?" she asked, a tear rolling down her face.

He wiped away the tear and kissed the top of her head. "Yes, but it's a temporary fix. I made enough to last a little while, a few weeks at most. And the effects won't last for more than an hour at a time, but you must work on yourself as well."

She gave a nod.

"Go on then, have a sip."

She removed the cork and drank the contents of the bottle. He could see a faint blue glow around her as it coursed through her body, seeping into every muscle. When it was empty, she smiled at him. Her eyes were dilated so far that the gray in her eyes was merely a sliver of a ring around them.

He felt how gleeful she suddenly was through their bond. He had almost forgotten that her arousal made the temperature rise. "And the water's gotten warmer," he laughed, taking the empty bottle from her. "Feeling better now?"

Again, she nodded, turning around in his lap with her usual luster in her gray eyes. "Much better, thank you," she grinned.

"And hungry, I see," he said with a raised brow.

"Mm hm," she replied, licking her full lips.

Before he could respond, she had descended on him. Her kiss was full of the fire and passion that he had missed. She could straddle him properly with his help, easing herself down on him. He inhaled sharply at how tight she was; he filled her completely. They made love in the bath as if they had been starving for one another. For the time being, he had his love back.

# CHAPTER 6

With the help of Roland's tincture, Kezia found the courage to see her son. Naturally, she was nervous about it. Connecting with Rhydian was going to be a challenge for her. She did not know what she was going to say to him.

There was a gentle knock at the door that pulled her out of her thoughts. A tall, lanky young man stepped into the room. His ears and face felt hot with nervousness when their eyes met, and he hesitated for a moment before going to her side. His face was a mixture of joy and uncertainty.

"Good day to you, mother." His voice cracked with emotion.

Kezia's heart ached as she looked up at her son, now just as tall as his father was. She reached out and pulled him into a tight embrace, feeling the warmth and strength of his body. "Rhydian, my sweet boy," she whispered, her tears soaking his shirt.

They held each other for what felt like an eternity, the years of separation melting away in that single moment.

Kezia pulled back slightly, cupping his face in her hands. "I'm so sorry I wasn't there for you," she said, her voice breaking. "I've missed so much."

Rhydian shook his head, his own eyes glistening with tears. "It's all right, mother. You're here now, and that's all that matters."

But it was not all right. It pained her to see how much he had grown without her there to witness it. "I should've been there for you growing up. I should've fed you, changed you, given you your first bath."

"Mother, really—"

"No, I wasn't there to read you stories or hear your first word. See you take your first steps," she continued, tears rolling down her face.

Rhydian sighed, kneeling in front of her. "Yes, you missed a lot, but it wasn't your fault. Just be here for me now. We'll sort the rest out later," he said with a warm smile.

Kezia smiled through her tears. She knew there would be challenges ahead, but she was determined to make up for lost time. "All right, I can do that. So, what would you like to do today?"

"I thought I'd take you up to the conservatory. There's someone there I'd like you to meet," he smiled.

She beamed up at him as he lifted her up to put her in her wheelchair. Once she was comfortably seated, they headed for the conservatory.

Varying aromas of herbs and flowers hit Kezia's senses upon arrival. It took her a few moments to get acclimated to such potent smells, but once she did, she marveled at the beauty and variety of the many plants. It was such a calming, serene part of the mansion outside of the garden.

"Beautiful, isn't it?" Rhydian spoke, interrupting her thoughts.

"It is," she replied. "Now, where is this young lady you'd like me to meet?"

Rhydian paled briefly. "About that—"

"Rhydian?" came a voice from behind them. "What are you doing up here? I thought you were spending the day with your mum."

"Yes," he replied, turning Kezia to face the other boy. "I wanted her to meet you properly."

Kezia looked up to see the equally tall and lanky boy her son was talking to. He looked familiar. She remembered he was in the room when she first woke up. When Rhydian walked over and kissed him, Kezia could not hide the surprise on her face.

"Mother, this is Dorian. My mate," he explained, smiling as he took hold of the other boy's hand.

"Oh!" she said. She blushed at the pair, her eyes still wide in shock, but then she smiled. "It's lovely to meet you, Dorian."

Rhydian breathed a sigh of relief, making Kezia giggle. "What's so funny?" he asked.

"You," she started. "There were a few men in my life that preferred other men as mates. You seemed worried that I wouldn't accept your relationship with Dorian."

Rhydian's face turned bright red with embarrassment.

"Did you forget we share a bond?" she laughed.

"Only briefly."

"Come here, Dorian. I wish to have a better look at you."

Dorian smiled and stepped forward. Kezia cupped his face and smiled, giving him a light pat on the cheek. He had soft brown eyes and long lashes that reminded her of an old friend. Even his skin, tanned from exposure to the sun, brought back memories of him.

"Back when I was an assassin, I had a friend named Sebastian who had a male mate. You remind me of him a little."

"That's funny. I had an uncle named Sebastian that had a male mate. I think his name was Michael. My mum said they died a long time ago, though."

Kezia frowned. They kicked Sebastian out of his pack when he chose Michael as his mate. He rarely spoke about his family, but she remembered he loved his sister. He had died on a mission before she took the contract to kill Roland. Michael hung himself shortly after.

"Oh, I'm sorry if I've upset you."

Kezia wiped a tear from her eye and shook her head. "No, it's all right. I wasn't aware he had a nephew."

"He died long before I was born. My mum used to talk about him a lot, though. Small world, I suppose," he shrugged.

"Indeed, it is," she agreed. She smiled wryly. It was such a long time ago, and she had forgotten that so much time had passed since then. Decades had gone by.

"You never told me you had an assassin for an uncle," said Rhydian.

Dorian laughed. "It never came up. He was an outcast, like me."

"Your pack expelled you?" Kezia asked. "Why?"

"I was too weak, but I have a new pack here, so I'm doing well now. Mum is happy about it."

"Yes, Ariel took him in over a year ago, and father put him to work," Rhydian explained.

"And I really like it here. I enjoy being around all the plants."

Kezia smiled warmly at him. "Sebastian was the same way."

Dorian took her by the hands. "You'll have to tell me all about him."

"Of course, I'd be happy to."

Rhydian smiled proudly. "I'm glad you two will get on well."

"How about we all have lunch?" Kezia suggested. "I'd like to know more about you both."

Dorian and Rhydian agreed, then they all went down to the dining hall together.


As they waited for their meals to arrive, Rhydian told Kezia how he learned control with Ariel's and Dorian's help. Kezia flushed with embarrassment. Even at fifty-eight, she had little control over her lust still. Roland was lucky to be immortal.

"Did your father ever tell you about Caelum?" she asked.

Rhydian shook his head. "Ariel told me about him."

Kezia scowled at that. How dare Roland not tell their son about Caelum. "I wish you could have met him. He was a good man. I miss him terribly."

"I heard about your training with him, though," said Rhydian.

Kezia laughed. "Oh, yes. That did not work out well for either of us. I suppose I was just too stubborn to learn."

They all had a good laugh when she explained in detail how her training went and how Caelum wound up bloodied and bruised for his efforts.

"There was another incubus that father introduced me to, Alvaro."

"Oh, I remember him!" she said. "Your father went to see him to ask for help while I was pregnant with you."

"I don't think he ever told me about that."

"Hm, it seems he hasn't told you about a lot of things," she growled, glaring at Roland when he walked in, followed by staff with their food.

"Uh oh. Am I in trouble?" he asked, taking a seat next to Kezia.

"You most certainly are," she grumbled when he laid a soft kiss on her cheek. "You have failed our son."

"Mother, please, don't be angry with him. I've already forgiven him for his neglect. He's been doing much better about it," Rhydian pleaded.

Kezia narrowed her eyes at Roland before turning her attention back to Rhydian. "Very well, I'll let it go. Why don't you tell me how you and Dorian met?"

Dorian perked up at that, his mouth full of food as he blushed. They all laughed, then Rhydian told her the brief story of how they met. He also told her about the disaster that was their first date, and how they were attacked by Dorian's cousin and his pack at the restaurant. Kezia was upset at first, but was relieved to know that Roland took care of things in the end.

They continued to talk and tell stories as they ate, doing their best to keep things light-hearted. Once they finished eating, Roland was called away by Lynnox to deal with a soul. With Dorian at his side, Rhydian pushed his mother along as they went for a walk, continuing to get to know each other. Kezia's heart swelled with pride and joy as she watched her son—he was becoming a fine young man, more than she could have ever hoped for. Yet the bittersweet sting of regret gnawed at her. The thought that she had missed so many precious moments of his childhood weighed heavily on her soul, each missed milestone a quiet ache she could not silence. The sadness cut deep, the guilt whispering that she had been absent when he needed her most. She vowed, with every fiber of her being, to spend the rest of her days making amends, pouring her love and devotion into his future. She would ensure he never again doubted how cherished he was, and that she would always nurture and celebrate his growth and joy.

# CHAPTER 7

oland's bond with his brother pulsed, a faint, almost imperceptible tug in his chest guiding him deeper into the darkened city. He had tracked his brother down before and always missed him. Left behind were brief notes, taunting Roland. Dorjan was aware of the bond as well. Though the bond was strong, his brother had regained his ability to travel through shadows and shape shift, which made it difficult for Roland to actually catch him. His heart pounded with a mix of anger and sorrow as he clutched the latest note from his twin. The words appeared, scrawled in a familiar, mocking script:

*Catch me if you can, dear brother. The shadows are my home now.*

The city was quiet, save for the occasional chirp of a cricket. It was late wherever he was, Roland was not sure. Dorjan was traveling from city to city, and country to country. He was looking for something he had lost. Roland scrutinized every sound and movement, his senses heightened. He could feel the bond pulling him towards a wooded area up ahead. As he approached, he saw a figure standing in the clearing, shrouded in shadows.

"Ozmir!" Roland called out, his voice echoing through the trees. "Face me!"

The figure turned, and for a moment, Roland saw his own face with green eyes and blond hair staring back at him. Dorjan's eyes gleamed with a mixture of mischief and malice.

"Ah, Zaven. Always so predictable," he said, his voice a whisper carried on the wind.

Roland tightened his fists. "This ends tonight, Ozzy. No more running."

Dorjan laughed. "You'll have to catch me first." With that, he melted into the shadows, his form dissipating like smoke.

Roland's frustration boiled over, but he forced himself to stay calm. He closed his eyes and focused on the bond. He could feel Dorjan's presence, a dark, elusive thread weaving through the shadows. Taking a deep breath, he followed, determined to end the nightmare that had torn his family apart.

As he followed his brother through the shadows, he could not shake the feeling that he was being watched. The shadows seemed to dance and flicker with an unnatural energy. He stopped his movements, listening to the silence.

"Who's there?" he called out.

Two figures emerged from the shadows. They were red-haired women, their movements elegant and effortless. Their eyes sparkled with mischief, and they wore identical smirks. Roland recognized them from the stories Luxor told him about his encounter with them. Dorjan's playful, yet dangerous familiars, the Mouras Encantadas.

"Well, well, look who we have here," one purred, her voice dripping with amusement.

"Poor Zaven, always chasing shadows," the other added, her tone equally teasing.

"Where's Ozmir?" he demanded, his eyes darting between the two women.

They exchanged a glance, their smiles widening.

"Where's the fun in telling you that?" one said, as her form glistened.

In an instant, both women shed their human forms, their bodies elongating and twisting into sleek, serpentine shapes that shimmered faintly in the dim light. Their movements were mesmerizing, a fluid dance of coiling and uncoiling that seemed to defy the boundaries of physical form. The air grew heavy with an almost tangible energy as they slithered around Roland, their scales glinting like liquid metal. Their eyes burned with an unearthly glow, sharp and predatory, locking onto him with an intensity that sent a shiver down his spine. The sound of their movements—a soft, rhythmic hiss—filled the space, amplifying the sense of danger and allure that radiated from them. It was as if the very air around them pulsed with an ancient, primal power, drawing him into their orbit, unable to look away.

"You'll have to get past us first," one said, her voice now a sibilant whisper.

Roland knew he had to stay focused. They were only trying to distract him. Delay the inevitable confrontation between him and his brother. But he knew the serpents were not just playful tricksters, they were formidable adversaries who would do anything to protect his brother. With a deep breath, Roland steadied himself and prepared to face the two familiars. His hunt was far from over.

As he readied himself, his eyes locked onto their serpentine forms as they circled him. The snakes moved with a fluid grace, their scales glinting in the moonlight. He knew he had to be cautious. The Mouras' playful demeanor masked their deadly nature. Though they could not kill him, their venom would still hurt and might put him down for a time.

One struck first, lunging at Roland with lightning speed. He barely had time to react, raising his hand to deflect her attack. She shrieked and recoiled, hissing in frustration. He had touched her snout and caused the blood in her face to explode into small spikes. The blow would not kill her, but it would injure her for some time. The other took advantage of the distraction and wrapped her tail around Roland's leg, trying to trip him up. He caught her tail, and blood exploded from it, severing the tip. She howled out and retracted the bloodied stump. It was becoming apparent that his brother failed to inform them he was a water elemental. Controlling blood was nothing to him.

"You can't stop me. I will find him," he growled.

The serpents exchanged another glance, their eyes gleaming with renewed amusement.

"Who said anything about stopping you?" one taunted, her form shifting back into a human shape. She stood before Roland, her hands glowing with dark, magical energy.

The other followed suit, transforming back into her human form as well. "We prefer to play," she said, her voice a seductive whisper.

Roland swore under his breath. Neither of them retained their injuries. "Enough games," he said, his voice resonating with authority. "I came here for Ozmir, and I will kill you to get to him if I have to."

Their expressions darkened, their playful demeanor fading.

"You think you can take him from us?" one snarled, her hands crackling with energy.

Roland tightened his fists. "I will do whatever it takes to stop him."

With a sudden burst of speed, they attacked in unison. Roland's water magic clashed with one's dark energy, while the other deflected it. The air crackled with magic as they battled. Roland could feel the bond with Dorjan pulsing, getting further away. He knew he had to end this quickly if he wanted to catch his brother.

With a powerful strike, Roland broke through one of their defenses, sending her sprawling to the ground.

"Bronagh!" the other shouted.

Roland sent the other flying in the opposite direction. He grabbed the one called Bronagh by the throat and lifted her up to meet his gaze.

"Where is he?" he demanded.

Bronagh glared at him, her eyes filled with defiance. "You'll never find him in time," she spat.

"What do you mean by that?" he growled out, tightening his hold.

"Wouldn't you like to know?" she wheezed, grinning.

Before he could react, her form shifted with a sickening fluidity, bones cracking and skin rippling beneath his fingers as she morphed back into a snake. In a flash, she lunged, her movement a blur of coiled muscle and deadly precision. He felt the sharp, searing pain as her fangs sank into his cheek, the venom burning like liquid fire as it spread. The hiss that followed was low and menacing, reverberating in his ears as the metallic tang of blood filled his senses. He dropped her as he held his face and screamed. All he heard were their fading cackles as they made their escape. He roared out in frustration, then froze when he felt Kezia's distress. Worry set in, and he raced to get back home.

When he arrived, he immediately went to their room, but found it empty. He went to Rhydian's room next. Empty.

"Kezia!" he called out in a panicked scream.

"Zaven?" came Lynnox's voice. "What on earth? Are ya all right?"

"Where is she?" he insisted.

"Who, love? Kezia?"

"Yes, and Rhydian."

"Oh, they're downstairs playin' games."

Roland closed his eyes and took a calming breath, then focused on the bond he shared with his wife and son. And, in an instant, he was gone again, leaving Lynnox confused in the hall. He reached the parlor room on the next floor and rushed to Kezia's side. He scooped her up in his arms and held her tight against him, getting a muffled protest from her.

"Put me down," she fussed. "What has gotten into you?"

"Nothing," he lied, putting her back in her chair. "I was just worried about you, is all."

"Why? I'm perfectly fine."

"I see that now. Sorry if I scared you."

She gave him a worried look. "Are you sure everything is all right? What's wrong?"

He smiled down at her, feeling her fear rise. "Yes, now that I'm back home with you."

She gave him another once over. "What happened to you? You've got blood on your face and hands. Why are there bite marks on your face?"

She was getting upset and freaking out. He needed to calm her down.

He touched his face and looked at his hands. "Oh, this? It's nothing. I'll go get cleaned up." He needed to recharge his energies. His wounds should have healed by now.

She and Rhydian exchanged worried looks. Now they were both panicking. He could feel it.

"You went after him again, didn't you?" Kezia asked.

"Really, I'm fine, you two," Roland said, avoiding the question. "Go back to your game. I'll be back in an hour or so."

"Roland—"

He interrupted her with a kiss, feeling her relax a little. When he let her go, he rubbed the dried bit of blood he had transferred to her cheek. They continued to stare worriedly as he turned to leave. He did not like lying to them, but he did not want to involve them in what he was doing. He had to find Dorjan before he regained his full power. But protecting his family from his brother was just as urgent. To restore his power, Dorjan needed to kill Kezia and Rhydian—something Roland would never allow.

# CHAPTER 8

*T*he air shimmered with divine energy as he stood at the center of the grand hall. He felt the weight of a thousand eyes upon him while he pled his case about the imbalance in the number of souls entering the underworld and the unrest it was causing. There were also breaches within the boundaries between the underworld and the mortal realm.

*Vala, resplendent in all her celestial glory, looked down at him from her throne with a mixture of disdain and disappointment. Her voice, cold and cutting, echoed through the hall as she berated him for his perceived failures.*

*"Ozmir, really. There is no imbalance," she declared, her words like daggers piercing his heart. "And how can*

*you call yourself a god if you can't quell a minor rebellion from souls?"*

*His siblings, each more radiant and powerful than the last, snickered and whispered amongst each other. He knew they had always seen him as weak, like he did not belong. That he was too softhearted.*

*One of his brothers, a god of war with a physique to match, stepped forward and sneered, "Maybe you should just give up, Ozmir. Leave the godly duties to those who can handle them."*

*Ozmir clenched his fists, his nails digging into his palms. He wanted to shout back, to defend himself, but the words caught in his throat. The hall seemed to close in around him, the divine light dimming as his confidence waned.*

*With Zaven on Earth living with his mortal woman, Ozmir felt more alone than ever. His twin had always been his shield, the one who stood up for him when no one else would. But now, in the grand hall, Ozmir had to face their mother's wrath and his siblings' mockery on his own.*

*Vala continued her tirade, her voice growing harsher with each word. "As for these rifts in the veil, your powers are more than sufficient to deal with them. If you're too weak for something so simple, I can always put another in your place. Perhaps your cousin Ma'or would be a better fit as guardian of the drowned."*

*The surrounding gods laughed, their voices a cruel chorus. Ozmir's heart ached, but he knew he could not rely on Zaven this time. He had to find his own strength. He took a deep breath, straightened his back, and met his mother's gaze. "I am not weak," he growled, his voice cutting through the laughter like a blade forged in defiance. "Caring does not diminish me. It is not a flaw—*

*it is my power. The strength to endure, to rise, and to fight comes not from apathy, but from the unrelenting will to protect."*

*The laughter faltered, and an uneasy silence settled as the gods shifted, surprised by the sudden force of his words.*

*Ozmir took a step forward. "I am more than my failures," he continued, his voice resolute. "They do not define me—they are a crucible that shaped me. And I will prove, not to you, but to myself, that I am worthy of my place among the gods."*

*Vala narrowed her eyes. But there was a flicker of something else—perhaps a hint of respect?*

Dorjan sneered at his memory. His mother and siblings never respected him. All because he cared too much. Now he would see them all pay for belittling him, and for punishing him for having interfered in a mortal's destiny. What was so special about Zaven that he got away with it so often?

Still hidden in the shadows, he watched as his brother fought his familiars. Dorjan was not worried that Roland would kill them. His brother had grown soft over the years because of his mortal family. He found the irony in that. They were his brother's weakness, but soon, they would no longer be an issue. He would recover all of his power before taking his revenge on his family.

Until that time, he would prepare himself for the fight with his brother. Dorjan was not aware of the blood bond carrying over to Rhianwen, though he should have suspected it sooner. His brother nearly caught him unawares the first time. Now he could use the bond to his advantage and stay ahead of him.

While Bronagh and Eadan kept his twin occupied, he would find the scale he had hidden on earth and have it fashioned into a weapon to kill a god. He knew he would be banished for what he had done to his brother's mortal woman, but he had hoped that Vala would not notice or care. He was wrong, of course, but at least he was prepared. The earth had shifted much since he was last in the celestial realm. There was a protective spell around his scale to keep it hidden from mortals and gods alike, but he had a rough idea of where he left it.

The spell he cast was intricate, requiring him to solve riddles and overcome challenges that would test his strength and wisdom. Along the way, he encountered creatures that could sense the faintest trace of the scale's magic. It left them corrupted and malformed. He had to dispatch several, and more appeared the closer he got to the scale. It was as if they were searching aimlessly for something they were not aware of.

As Dorjan pushed past the twisted, corrupted creatures, their ragged breaths and guttural growls fading into the distance, he stood before a labyrinth that seemed to rise from the earth itself. The air grew heavier, thick with an unexplainable energy, and the maze loomed before him— its dark, winding corridors stretching endlessly, their walls pulsating faintly as though the structure were alive. Jagged stones, reflecting dim, flickering light from an indiscernible source, lined the path, casting eerie, shifting shadows that played tricks on his eyes.

Almost immediately, the illusions began. The scent of flowers long dead mingled with the acrid tang of smoke, and distant whispers curled around him like unseen fingers, tugging at the edges of his sanity. The walls seemed to ripple and shift, their surfaces morphing into shapes of leering faces or familiar places that beckoned him forward. Footfalls echoed unnaturally, sometimes doubling back as if someone—or something—was following in his steps.

Dorjan struggled to separate reality from the phantoms conjured by the labyrinth. At times, the floor beneath his feet seemed to drop away, leaving him momentarily weightless until his magical senses affirmed it was merely a cruel illusion. His hands reached out, fingertips brushing the cold, rough stone walls, searching for some anchor to the real. The rhythmic thrum of his heartbeat, which seemed to grow louder with each wrong turn, broke the oppressive silence.

He relied on his intuition and the faint hum of his magical abilities, which pulsed softly in his chest, acting like a fragile compass in this world of shifting deception. Every step forward was a battle of will, each choice a test of his resolve to outmatch the maze's ever-changing traps.

Dorjan grew more frustrated as he moved further into the labyrinth. Walls, carved from polished obsidian, lined one path; their surfaces reflected faint, distorted images of Dorjan as he moved. The air here shimmered with an unnatural heat, like a mirage, and the floor beneath his feet seemed to ripple, creating the illusion of walking on liquid. Whispers rose and fell like a phantom choir, promising safety just beyond the next turn.

Another path had thick, gnarled roots that broke through the stone floor, their dark tendrils curling like grasping fingers. The air smelled of damp earth and decaying foliage, and a faint, greenish glow emanated from patches of bioluminescent moss clinging to the walls. The path pulsed with life, but it felt more like a predator watching from the shadows than a sanctuary.

Each path he took would seal itself to prevent him from advancing forward, and force him to double back and find a new one. He tried burning his way through the hedges and stone walls, but his fire could not penetrate the magical barriers. He cursed under his breath. Vala must have had her Emori agents erect the dreadful obstacle. Wiping the entirety of the Emori out would be thoroughly enjoyable.

As he continued, the illusions became auditory. He was hearing voices now—and one was laughing.

"You will fail," the voice whispered. "You are weak, and you will fail."

"I don't make a habit of listening to phantoms," Dorjan said flatly. "Especially ones that aren't real."

"Oh, but I am very real," it purred.

Dorjan stopped walking, and with an expression of pure exasperation, he said, "Then show yourself so I can kill you."

"Well, that would be suicide," it said. "Wouldn't it?"

With the same tired expression, Dorjan saw a figure he recognized immediately. The figure had short, platinum blond hair and wicked blue eyes. He had almost forgotten what color his eyes used to be. It was an illusion, of course, a shadow of who he once was before he was banished to the mortal realm.

"So, this is what we're doing?" He stepped around the apparition and continued on his path.

His shadow self in his god form gleefully followed, catching up to walk beside him.

"I hope you know you're going the wrong way," his shadow self grinned.

Dorjan sighed. "If you insist on tagging along, I ask that you be silent."

"Now where's the fun in that?" it laughed. "You don't have to listen. I'm not real. Remember?"

Dorjan walked faster. The sooner he got to his scale, the better. He knew the spell he cast around it could not be removed by anyone other than him.

"Oh, Ozmir, you can't run from me," it said, floating in a circle around him. "You can't hide from the truth. You think you're a hero, but deep down, you know you're just a scared, broken little boy who hates his mother."

"I believe nothing of the sort," he replied, his voice indifferent.

"You're weak, Ozmir. And you always will be."

"I am not now, nor have I ever been weak," he growled.

Again, the illusion grinned. "Then prove it. Face me, and face the truth about yourself. Only then will you find your way through the labyrinth."

Dorjan stopped again, exhaling through his nose. "Fine, have it your way."

His shadow self narrowed its eyes. "So, you have some fight in you, after all. Interesting."

"Out with it, phantom! I haven't all night."

"I told you, I'm not a phantom," it smirked. "I am you, Ozmir. I am the part of you that you try to bury deep inside. Your fears, your doubts," it continued. "Your darkest thoughts," it said in his face as it smiled broadly.

"You're just an illusion built into a spell in this cursed labyrinth."

"I am as real as the fear that you'll never be strong enough. Good enough."

"I'm not listening to your nonsense," he sneered, then started walking again.

"That determination won't save you, Ozzy," it called after him. "You must embrace your darkness, not just fight it." It appeared in an instant in front of him.

Dorjan grinned at that. "Fool, I am the darkness." With that, he conjured his fire and set the illusion ablaze.

Instead of screaming, it cackled. "The labyrinth hasn't finished with you yet."

The fire ate up the illusion of his god form until the flames went out, leaving behind the echoes of laughter. Dorjan pressed on.

The next path he took, the stones were jagged and uneven, as if some violent force had shattered it. The walls glowed faintly with cracks of molten light, spilling a warmth that was both comforting and threatening. Occasionally, the ground would tremble beneath Dorjan's feet, and the sound of distant, echoing crashes hinted at the shifting nature of this path, as if it might collapse entirely at any moment. He hurried out of that path as quickly as he could, not trusting that it would remain intact.

After another hour or more, and many frightening paths later, he came upon an open area. On the other side was a small tomb structure, and guarding it were a pair of Alphyn.

Dorjan groaned, approaching the beasts. "Let me guess, I have to fight you both?"

"No, demon, but you must answer two riddles to unlock the doors," said the one on the right.

"Or I could just kill you both and burn the doors down," he offered. He was tired of his mother's games. Then he remembered he had set this up.

"You could," the other smiled. "But you will fail and the door will vanish, along with your scale."

Dorjan had a look of utter disdain. He closed his eyes and took a calming breath. "Fine, tell me your riddles."

The one on the right went first. "I am not alive, but I grow. I do not have lungs, but I need air; I do not have a mouth, and yet I can drown. What am I?"

Dorjan glared menacingly. He was beyond tired and had no desire to play games. He did not want to make things easy in case someone else stumbled upon his scale, but he wanted to be out of this wretched place sooner rather than later. The urge to set the beast on fire was strong. Then the answer came to him, and he felt like a fool for not realizing it sooner. "The answer is fire."

With his answer, Dorjan watched as a locking spell disengaged on the doors. Then the Alphyn on the right disappeared.

"I speak without a mouth and hear without ears. I have no body, but I come alive with the wind. What am I?" asked the remaining Alphyn.

The riddle challenged Dorjan's perception and understanding of the intangible. "You are an echo," he answered.

With his answer, the second locking spell disengaged, and the other Alphyn disappeared. At last, the doors opened, and there, floating above a pedestal, was a glowing orb. Inside the orb was a large white scale with golden trim and details. Before he stepped forward into the tomb, he looked around for traps. He was far too tired to deal with anything else his vile mother had lying in wait for him.

When he saw nothing suspicious, he cautiously stepped inside the tomb, his movements deliberate and quiet, as if the silence itself might shatter and awaken some unseen danger. The air inside was heavy, thick with a kind of ancient magic that seemed to swirl around him in unseen currents. His hands trembled slightly as he began the intricate ritual of removing the spells binding the scale. The room seemed to pulse with his every word, the magic reluctantly unraveling, thread by thread, as he chanted.

Finally, the scale—an object of impossible beauty and power—rested in his hands. Its surface shimmered, catching the dim light in unnatural ways, as though the scale itself breathed and responded to his touch. For a moment, time seemed to stop, and the weight of his achievement settled over him. But just as the thought took root, the world shifted violently.

The walls of the tomb crumbled as if struck by an unseen force, the debris disintegrating into nothingness before it hit the ground. And the labyrinth that had ensnared him and tested his will vanished without a trace, leaving behind a clearing drenched in eerie silence. The air was dry and brittle, carrying the faint scent of ash and decay.

He turned slowly, taking in the desolate landscape. The forest around him stretched endlessly, its dead trees twisted and hollow, their bare branches clawing at the dark sky like skeletal fingers. The ground beneath him was cracked and barren, its color drained as if the life force of the earth had been devoured. A sense of dread hung heavy, and though he had escaped the labyrinth, he could not shake the feeling that this forest might offer a fate far worse.

He smiled broadly at the scene before him, then vanished into the shadows.

# CHAPTER 9

The following morning, the weather was calm. Although there was the threat of rain with clouds forming, they were not rolling, turbulent harbingers of doom. With Roland away on business, Rhydian readily stepped in to assist Kezia with her physical therapy for the day. The golden sunlight, what little there was of it, streamed through the soft lace curtains, bathing the room in a gentle, amber glow that seemed to soften the edges of everything it touched. Rhydian moved with a quiet precision, carefully helping his mother into a comfortable position, his hands steady yet tender. Kezia offered a faint, grateful smile, her eyes reflecting a mixture of determination and the undeniable weariness of her journey. He was just as nervous. He was not sure what to expect. She grabbed a small satchel from the nightstand next to the bed; the contents clinking slightly as she secured it to her person. For a moment, the only sounds in the room were the faint rustle of fabric and the distant melody of birdsong filtering in through the open window. Gently, he helped her ease herself into the wheelchair, then he pushed her along to what he was told was once her combat training room.

As they made their way to the room, Rhydian was lost in thought. He was still amazed to know that his mother was a former assassin, of all things. It amused him to know that was how his parents met. He could not imagine such an awkward yet wonderful surprise for his birthday. Though his father was lucky to be immortal. From the sound of things, his mother was fierce and skilled. Rhydian had high hopes for her therapy session.

"My darling, you passed the room," Kezia giggled.

"Hm? Oh! Sorry, mother," he blushed, embarrassed that he was not focused. This was not the time to be daydreaming, he thought. He had to be on task for his mother.

She smiled up at him as he turned her around and headed back in the right direction. "Where were you just now?"

Again, his face turned red with embarrassment. "I was just thinking about how you and father met. I find it all so fascinating."

"Really?" She had a nervous look in her eyes. "What all did he tell you about the encounter?"

"That you were disguised as a dancer, and that you were the most beautiful woman he had ever seen... then you tried to murder him," he smiled. "He was a little vague about the details, though."

"Of course he was," she said with a smile and a look of relief on her face.

He narrowed his eyes at her, wondering what his father left out that would make her nervous. He made a mental note to ask her about it later. They were in her therapy room and they needed to focus on that.

Once inside, they set her satchel aside, and he gave the place a once over. The room was large and open, giving them ample space to work. There was a set of wooden parallel bars mounted to the hardwood floors to support her while she practiced walking, a thin rug between them for her comfort. He noticed her glaring at them.

"Why don't we start with some warm-up exercises before we get to the bars?" Rhydian offered.

Kezia gave a curt nod in agreement.

Rhydian guided her through slow rotations of her wrists, ankles, and shoulders to ease stiffness and improve her range of motion. When she winced, she had him go into her satchel and give her a bottle of a strange, translucent liquid that had a faint blue shimmer to it. She quickly drank the substance, and her whole body relaxed and she had the same faint blue shimmer as it coursed through her.

He took the empty bottle from her and set it down on the floor, a confused look on his face. "What was that stuff, mother?"

"It was a tincture your father made for me to help make things easier while I recover," she explained, her face bright and giddy. "It's made with mermaid tears."

"Oh, all right then. Shall we continue?"

She nodded again, and she seemed almost drunkenly happy. It gave him cause for concern. He knew mermaid tears were good for elevating one's mood and to heal minor internal wounds, but he had never heard of it having the effect that it seemed to have on his mother. Still, he trusted his father would not have given her something that might be harmful to her, so they continued with her warm-ups.

With gentle, steady hands, Rhydian supported his mother as she stretched out her legs, guiding each movement with care. Her muscles, tight and unyielding at first, slowly relaxed under the patient rhythm of his touch. He moved to her arms, encouraging her through small, deliberate stretches, the tension easing little by little as he focused on every subtle shift in her body. The warmth of his palms against her skin and the calm precision of his movements created a soothing flow, each motion designed to coax her muscles into soft pliancy. He guided her movements with steady hands, his encouraging smile never faltering. The minutes ticked by, his gentle instructions weaving seamlessly with her growing confidence. Around the thirty-minute mark, he gave a satisfied nod and reached for a small stress ball. Rhydian provided Kezia with the small, padded ball to squeeze in order to help her build up the strength in her hands and forearms.

"Let's work on grip strength now," he said, watching as her fingers hesitated before slowly wrapping around the ball.

Again, she winced, and this time, she cried out. The ball landed with a thud as it hit the hardwood floor.

"Mother! Are you all right?" he asked worriedly.

She held her forearm close to her chest and nodded. "I'm sorry, my darling. I just overdid it a little. It was not my intention to worry you."

He frowned. "Are you certain?"

"Yes, but can you hand me another bottle of the tincture? It seems to wear off rather quickly."

"Of course." He handed her another bottle and she once again downed it quickly.

After some seated assisted leg lifts, she wanted to move on to the parallel bars.

"You seem to be having trouble today. Are you sure you want to try them?" he asked, his tone even, but concerned.

"Oh, yes!" she replied gleefully. "I think I can handle walking a bit today."

"All right, but you'll let me know if it gets to be too much?"

"Yes, yes. Of course I will," she said, waving him off.

With a sigh, he wheeled her over to the bars. He gingerly helped her out of the chair, holding her arm gently as she gripped the bars with trembling hands. Her knuckles were pale against the dark wood as she steadied herself, her breath shallow and quick.

"Take it slow," he murmured, his tone calm but encouraging. "Focus on each step, not the distance ahead."

She hesitated, staring down at her bare feet. He thought they must have felt foreign to her, as if they belonged to someone else. After sixteen years of stillness, it must have felt like every muscle was straining against a chain. At least he imagined so. He had no way of knowing how she actually felt. The magical bond they shared only let him know she was feeling uneasy about all of this, but not anything physical for once.

Summoning all her will, Kezia took one halting step forward, her left foot barely lifting off the floor. She placed down, and then her right foot lifted from the ground. She took another couple of steps before a sharp, involuntary gasp escaped her lips as she shifted her weight. The bar creaked faintly under her grip. Her body wavered for just a moment, and Rhydian tightened his hold on her just enough to steady her.

Then she stopped, her breathing turning shallow and uneven. He could see her frustration bubble over and she suddenly cried out.

"No, I can't do this! It's hopeless. I'm... hopeless."

Rhydian took a deep breath, his expression conflicted but caring. "Mother," he said softly, "look behind you."

Reluctantly, she did. The smallest of footprints—just a few—rested on the rug beneath the bars, marking her progress. It was barely a few steps, but they were hers. Tears welled in her eyes, and for a moment, her grip loosened on the bars.

"You're not hopeless," he said, his voice firm, but full of warmth. "You've already come further than you think."

She turned her head away, refusing to look at him. "It's useless," she spat out, frustration sharpening her words. "Sixteen years... Sixteen years and I'm left like this. I was an assassin! And a Grimnir at that!"

Rhydian straightened up. "You're stronger than you think," he said firmly. "Just try again. You've done it once before with father."

"Fine," she sighed. "But hand me another bottle first."

"You've had two already. Does it really wear off so quickly?" he asked. He genuinely wanted to know. The substance was strange to him. Mermaid tears did not glow like that, and they did not wear off so quickly.

"Your father said that each bottle would last an hour, possibly, but I've been using it for a few days and the time has gotten shorter."

"I see. Surely you can do this without that stuff."

She gritted her teeth. "Rhydian Drake, do as I say," she growled out. "Please," she said after a moment, adjusting her tone.

He hesitated, giving her another worried look, before going over to retrieve the satchel of bottles. He watched her drink down two of the bottles this time. She glowed brighter, and with renewed vigor, she straightened herself up and tightened her grip on the bars. She took another couple of unsteady steps, and then more, until she reached the end of the path. When she turned to him, she was all smiles and practically vibrating with excitement. Rhydian wanted to be happy for her, but she did not do it on her own like he had hoped she would. He returned her smile, but knew he would have to have a talk with his father about her abuse of the tincture he made for her. It was affecting her in an odd way, and he worried about her health.

# Chapter 10

As the music began, a haunting melody that echoed through the tent, Aiden watched as Raesh launched himself into the air, his wings unfurling in a dramatic display of fire and feathers. Raesh soared above the arena, his silhouette cutting through the dim light. With a swift motion, he drew his knives.

With every knife thrown, Sacha's powers came to life. She raised walls of earth to catch the knives, then let them crumble back to the ground. The knives flew faster and closer, each one a testament of their trust and skill. The crowd gasped and cheered as the show went on.

Raesh and Sacha had dazzled audiences for years with a variety of breathtaking stunts, each showcasing their unique abilities and the deep trust between them. Aiden was proud to have them among his troop. He knew his father would be as well.

Aiden watched as the pair took their bows and left the arena. He went back to his trailer. He had sent a page to summon Raesh to him. There was something important he was reluctant to discuss with him. The circus had received a summons for a private performance. While that was a welcomed surprise, the requestor was what worried him.

Aiden did not want to accept the offer. He suspected it was an Emori trap being set for Raesh. But Roland Ausher was a businessman, a husband, and a father... and most importantly, a god of death. He had never liked the Emori and refused to help them in their missions to capture Raesh. However, his wife had, and she was no longer in a coma.

"You wanted to see me?" came Raesh's voice, pulling Aiden out of his thoughts.

"Yes, Andy. Come in, please," he answered solemnly, offering Raesh the seat in front of his desk.

"If this is about our finances, and how expensive Korlue is—"

Aiden held up his hand to silence him. "It is about our finances, but has nothing to do with Korlue."

Raesh sat down and stared quietly at Aiden, and for a moment, Aiden thought he saw concern in the dragon's eyes.

"Well, what is it?"

"Right. How long has it been since you last saw an Emori agent?" Aiden asked.

Raesh narrowed his eyes. "A week ago. I killed him. Why do you ask?"

"Andrew! Really?" he fussed, disappointment in his tone.

Raesh stared at him with an apathetic look in his eyes. "This line of questioning cannot possibly have any bearing on our finances."

"Actually, it might. About a week ago, we got an invitation to do a private performance," he said with reluctance.

"I still do not see the correlation," Raesh admitted. "What are you getting at?"

"It was from Roland Ausher."

It was the first time Aiden had seen fear in the dragon. He sat there frozen, eyes wide, but it was a brief, fleeting moment. His expression quickly changed to anger.

"Why am I only hearing about this now?" he demanded, his power flaring and filling the small room with the distinct odor of sulfur.

"Because of how you're acting now," Aiden replied calmly, pulling at his shirt collar. It had gotten warmer in the room. "I didn't want to upset you."

Raesh took a deep calming breath and let the temperature in the room even back out. "Ausher and I have a history. You should have told me right away."

"Oh, I'm more than aware of your past with Roland Ausher. The Emori were keeping tabs on him long before you met him. It's not often a god decides to live among us mortals," he said, pulling out a bottle of cheap whiskey and two glasses.

Raesh respectfully declined the offer of a drink. Aiden shrugged and poured himself a glass.

"What will you do?" Raesh asked. "About the invitation?"

"I haven't accepted it," he replied, taking a drink. "And I don't think I will. While he is offering a large sum of money, I can't risk it not being a trap for you."

"But the circus could use the funds, correct?"

"Yes," Aiden nodded. "But we need you more."

"I understand your attachment, but I am no longer a killer for hire. My fortune has long since dried up. You should accept the offer."

"Kezia is no longer in a coma. What if they mean to harm you?" Aiden asked worriedly. "No, I won't take that chance. We make enough to live modestly."

"Is this not a circus of reformed killers?" Raesh smiled.

"Mostly. You did just admit to killing a man a week ago," he replied, finishing his drink, and then pouring himself another. "What of it?"

"If it is indeed a trap for me, we can fight. The Emori are weak, but what if it is not a trap?"

"Do you really want to take that chance?" Aiden eyed Raesh carefully as the dragon thought on it. Aiden agreed it might not be a trap. Roland Ausher might just want to celebrate his wife's awakening as the invite said, but he seriously doubted it. Why would he want to put his wife in the same place as her abuser? And the offer just seemed too good to be true.

"Aiden?" Raesh called.

"Hm? Oh, sorry. You were saying?"

"I was saying that this circus is my family, and while I do not wish to endanger you more than I already have, I think we should go," he explained. "I will stay behind just in case it is a trap."

Aiden shook his head. "No, you and Sacha are the headliners. He's paying for you to come out there."

"Then I suggest we put on the best show and prepare for a fight."

"I'd rather you go back to being a killer for hire," Aiden laughed.

"That is out of the question," Raesh retorted.

"Fine, fine. We'll go, but I suggest you sharpen that killer instinct before we do."

Raesh smirked. "This will be a most interesting adventure."

# CHAPTER 11

R aesh stepped out of Aiden's trailer, his mind
still buzzing with the conversation they had.
He could not believe after all this time that
Kezia had woken up from her long coma. He felt bad for
trying to kill her, especially when she was with child.
There were a great many things he regretted doing to her,
but she wound up having a good life with her new mate.
Until her coma, that is.

As he reentered the main tent to watch the remainder of
the show, he almost collided with Sacha.

Her eyes sparkled with a mix of surprise and
amusement. He was usually more aware of his
surroundings, but he was lost in his thoughts. Perhaps
Aiden was right. He should work on his killer instinct.

"Andrew! What are you doing back here?" she asked with a grin.

"I wanted to watch the others perform," he replied.

"Oh, well, you're not missing anything. The clowns are being their usual silly selves," she told him. "Care to take a walk with me?" She asked, gesturing out of the tent.

"If you insist," he answered, falling in step beside her.

As they walked, Raesh glanced down at her. He could see the fine gray hairs that peppered her dark tresses in the moonlight. She really was getting older, and she never got over Lucas' death. He imagined them marrying and having children if Lucas had not been murdered. She deserved a peaceful life with a family. "You know, you have never actually told me much about your life before the circus. What was it like for you, being a mercenary?"

Sacha's expression softened, and she let out a small sigh. "It was... intense. I was an orphan, and I started young, just a slip of a girl. It was dangerous work, but it paid well. I traveled a lot, saw places most people only dream about. But it was lonely. And trust was a rare commodity in that line of work, but you know all that."

He nodded, listening intently. "What made you leave it all behind?"

She smiled wistfully. "I grew tired of the constant fighting and the endless cycle of violence. One day, I stumbled upon a traveling circus. It was smaller then, but everyone was full of life and laughter. It felt like a place where I could finally belong. So, I took a leap of faith and joined them."

Raesh smiled, feeling a deeper connection with her. "I am glad you did. The circus would not be the same without you."

Sacha chuckled. "Thank you. I could say the same about you. You have changed quite a lot since you joined. Though you're still very grumpy."

He frowned at that. "I am not grumpy."

Again, she laughed, and he realized he had proven her point.

"So, why don't you tell me about this Korlue person? You never talk about him."

Raesh's eyes widened in surprise briefly. He had brought up Korlue once with her, and that was only when he went to go see him after practice. She had never asked about him after that.

"Come on, don't be shy," she grinned, bumping into his side playfully. "I'm your partner, after all."

"Did Aiden put you up to this?" he asked, narrowing his eyes at her.

It would be just like the nosy blond to send someone else to ask about his personal life. Raesh had refused to share such intimate things with anyone.

"What? No!" she said, feigning offense. "But he did tell me you claimed Korlue as your mate. That's a pretty big deal for you."

"Is it?" he inquired, genuinely curious.

"Yes! You're such a loner. I never thought you, of all people, would ever have a mate."

Raesh took mild offense to that. He had many lovers before Korlue, but he never actually cared for any of them. Not like he did Korlue. Not Zahira. Or even Ivy. "I see," he said. "All right, what would you like to know?"

He almost immediately regretted his words when her entire face lit up.

"Tell me everything! What's he like?"

Raesh sighed, then proceeded to tell her all that he knew of Korlue. How he was kind and gentle, but exceedingly clumsy and trusted too easily. Korlue loved to read and collect books. He was a fan of the arts and enjoyed going to shows, such as operas, dramas, and ballets. Things that Raesh did not enjoy, but it made Korlue happy and that was what he cared about. Seeing Korlue happy and being with him almost made him a better person.

Sacha beamed up at him. "You glow when you talk about him."

"I do not glow," he scowled.

"You are such a sourpuss!" she laughed. "But I'm glad he makes you happy."

"Thank you."

"When do you think you'll settle down with him? You can't live with the circus forever."

Raesh grumbled. "Perhaps we should be getting back. The show will be over soon."

She narrowed her eyes at him but said nothing more about it. They walked back to the main tent, mostly in silence. It gave Raesh time to think about things. He cared a great deal for his mate, but he never thought about quitting the circus and settling down with him. It was a grand thought of a life he did not think he could ever have, or one that he even deserved. Especially since he spent the better part of two centuries murdering people.

He found himself wondering if spending the rest of his days with him was something Korlue even wanted. What if Korlue rejected him? He had never actually told Korlue that he thought of him as his mate. The thought worried him. Korlue had become accustomed to a certain lifestyle. How would he keep up with his wants and needs?

"Drew?" Sacha called, a worried look on her face. "Is everything all right?"

"Hm? Oh, yes. I am fine," he smiled down at her. "Just lost in my thoughts."

"Should I be worried?"

"No," he replied, opening the curtain for her to enter.

She hesitated before patting his chest, then going in.

Raesh took a moment before following her. He would talk things over with Korlue the next time he saw him.

# CHAPTER 12

Once he took his mother back to her room to rest for the day, Rhydian went in search of his father. He had heard that he was back in Wales that afternoon. The first place he looked was his office, not surprised to see him there. Roland was scribbling away in a large leather book when Rhydian knocked on the open door.

"Rhydian? What are you doing here?" he asked, closing the book and pushing it aside. "Is something the matter?"

"Yes, actually. We need to talk about mother."

Roland furrowed his brow. "What about her? Is she all right?"

Rhydian sighed. "Physically, yes, but emotionally, I'm not entirely sure. During her session today, I noticed her needing to use a tincture you made for her, and it seems like she's relying on it too much."

"What do you mean? The tincture is meant to help her with her therapy," he said, giving Rhydian his full attention.

"I assumed as much, and I'm grateful for that. But it's like she's abusing it. She's taking it frequently and I'm worried it will affect her mood and behavior," he explained.

"Hmm, I see. I should have expected this to happen. The tincture was supposed to be a temporary aid, not something she was supposed to depend on. I infused it with my energy to strengthen it, and she has a bit of an addiction to my essence," he sighed. He sounded frustrated.

Rhydian had a look of disappointment on his face. "We need to do something before it gets worse. Maybe we can talk to her and help her understand any risk of overusing it."

"You're right, son," he said, scratching at his overgrown beard. "I'll have a talk with her about it later."

"Father, this is serious. I think we should both talk to her, and we should do it sooner rather than later."

"I understand the urgency, Rhydian, but now is not a good time. This is a delicate matter, and she has a horrible temper. We need to discuss tactics before confronting her," Roland explained calmly. "She's prone to throwing sharp things."

Rhydian took a deep breath. His father was right. A level head was needed for an addiction intervention.

Especially when dealing with a former coma patient that was once an assassin.

Still, Rhydian stared at his father with disdain. His mother had a problem, and Roland was acting like it was no big deal.

"Have a seat, son," he said, motioning for him to sit in the chair in front of his desk. "Why don't you tell me what happened today?"

Rhydian hesitated briefly, but went and sat down as instructed. He relayed the events of that morning with his mother and her physical therapy session. What looked like concern and guilt washed over Roland's face as Rhydian spoke of Kezia's use of the tincture. Though he was reluctant to admit it, Roland was concerned about the sudden addiction. He had only meant for the tincture to help improve Kezia's mood and do some minor internal healing. They went over what they would say to her about her dependency. An intervention was a hard thing for a family, especially one like theirs, but it needed to be done. It was for her own good. They would wait until she was better rested and in a mood to hear their concerns for her.

When Kezia finally woke up from her nap, Rhydian went to retrieve her. He offered to take her to the gardens for a bit of fresh air, but she declined. Instead, she wanted to hear more about his life growing up. Rhydian was happy to oblige her and even offered to teach her how to play cards. It was something that he picked up in London that he and Dorian enjoyed. She agreed, excited to get to know her son better. Rhydian felt a pang of guilt for not telling her what was about to happen, but when she grabbed her satchel of tinctures, he let the feeling go. She needed to know that she did not need a crutch to get better. Not when she had her family.

Roland had told Rhydian that he would bring up the subject of her addiction with Kezia. The last thing he wanted was for her to be angry with her son. Not when they were getting to know each other. And Roland was more accustomed to her temper. Rhydian gratefully agreed.

He took her to the den, and they began their game of gin. She was surprisingly good at it, and it was not long before she was beating him at the game.

"I win again!" she squealed happily. "I think I like this game."

Rhydian smiled warmly. "I'm glad you're having fun, mother."

She narrowed her eyes at him. "What's the matter? I've been sensing an odd feeling from you since I woke up from my nap. You're not letting me win, are you?"

"No! I would never do something so underhanded," he said, his tone even, but somewhat offended. "Especially not to you."

"Well, then, what's on your mind, my darling?" she inquired.

Before he could answer, Roland came into the room. Kezia scowled at her husband for interrupting their moment together.

"Shoo!" she fussed. "Rhydian and I are spending some much-needed time together."

Roland glowered at her. "I'm here because I need to be. Something serious has been brought to my attention, love."

Her expression turned serious. "Is something the matter? Should I be worried, too?"

Roland sighed, taking a seat on the large sofa. "Yes, actually."

"What on earth is going on with you two?" she asked, her voice slightly panicked. "Is it about my father?"

"No, love. It's about you."

She looked taken aback by his admission. "Is there something wrong with me?"

Rhydian took a deep breath before answering her. "No, mother. We're just worried about you."

"Whatever for?" she asked, facing her son.

She had a look of panicked confusion on her face as she turned back to her husband. Roland had talked about her temper more than once, and Rhydian was worried now. He quietly removed the playing cards from her reach, thinking their sharp edges could be used as projectiles. His father did say she was prone to throwing sharp things.

"It's about your use of the tincture," Roland said. "I have been told that you're taking too much of it."

Again, she scowled at her husband. "You made it for me to use as needed. And that is all I use it for." Her tone had taken on a defensive inflection.

"Yes, but you're taking it for every minor pain or setback," Rhydian explained. "I saw how many bottles you went through today."

"How would you know how minor my pain is? I'm the one that feels it!" she snapped. She covered her mouth, surprised at her own words. "I'm sorry, my darling. I didn't mean to yell at you."

"You're almost out, aren't you?" Roland asked. He was surprisingly calm.

Kezia clutched the satchel close to her protectively. "I have plenty left."

"Then let me see the bag, Kezia," Roland insisted.

"Why? What if I need it?"

"You don't need it all the time, love. It's supposed to be temporary. When you run out, I won't make anymore for you," he said. "I told you that you're going to have to work on yourself while using the tincture, but you haven't been."

"I'm in no mood to be lectured by someone who couldn't even control his emotions well enough to raise his son!" she barked.

The room fell silent for a few moments as Kezia's words hung in the air. They were all stunned into silence, none of them sure of what to say next. It was Kezia who finally spoke first.

"Rhydian, I'm tired now. Take me back to my room," she said.

Rhydian sat there another moment, staring at his mother in disbelief. "No," he answered. "Not until you apologize to father and admit you have a problem."

She narrowed her eyes at her son, an incredulous look on her face. "Why should I apologize? It's true. I've heard the servants whispering about how much of a drunken mess he was. He neglected you."

"Yes, but he was trying to do better before you woke up. I've forgiven him for all of that already," he said. "Now, apologize to him."

"Rhydian, it's all right. She doesn't have to," Roland said solemnly. "She's right. I couldn't face my demons well enough to raise you proper. And for that, I'm truly sorry."

"Father..."

"But there's nothing that can be done to change the past," Roland continued. "Kezia, you have a problem, but you can't even admit to it."

"I don't have a problem. I'm fine."

"Then give me what's left of the tincture," he insisted, his tone gentle but firm.

"But I need it."

"No, you don't. Can't you see how it's affecting you? You've become dependent on it."

"How can you say that?"

Roland sighed, grumbling. "You lashed out at Rhydian and just attacked me, Kezia. I know this is my fault, but if you were fine, you wouldn't have done that."

Rhydian watched as his parents fought, a sad look on his face. He was not sure what to say or do next. He had not thought to move the vase sitting on the table near her until it was hurled at his father. She had aimed at his head, and the porcelain shattered on his face, leaving small slivers of the vase in his skin. He sighed and casually pulled them out one by one, the wounds healing instantly.

"Mother!" Rhydian shouted.

She opened her mouth to speak, then closed it. "I'm sorry," she muttered, looking away from them.

Rhydian could hear the shame in her voice, but there was still some defiance in her eyes. "Please, mother. Let us have the tinctures."

She hugged the bag close again. Then, after a moment, she let it go, handing the satchel to Roland. He took it gingerly, his eyes never leaving Kezia's.

"I'm sorry, love. I never meant for this to happen," he murmured.

A tear ran down her cheek and she sniffled. "I'm sorry, too. I mean it this time."

Rhydian breathed a sigh of relief. "Did you still want to go back up to your room, mother?"

She nodded, not trusting her voice.

"I'll take her up," Roland offered. "If that's all right with you, Kezia?"

She looked up at her husband, unshed tears shining in her eyes. "Please. I think we should talk in private."

Roland handed the satchel of tinctures over to Rhydian. "Put these away for now. I'll deal with them later."

Rhydian nodded, taking the bag. He watched as his father wheeled his mother away. He still felt bad, as if he had deceived her somehow. It left him wondering if he had made a big deal out of nothing. She would have run out of the tincture eventually, and Roland would not have made anymore for her. He was sure that would have upset her, but not to the point of yelling and throwing things at her husband. Of course, he knew very little about their relationship.

"Oh, to be a fly on that wall," spoke a familiar baritone.

Rhydian turned to see Luxor lounging on the large sofa that Roland had just got up from. He appeared out of nowhere.

"Hello, Luxor. What do you mean by that?" Rhydian asked, his voice holding a hint of concern.

"Nothing for you to worry about, lad," he said, a casual look on his face. "Your parents will be fine when this is all over."

"How can you be so sure?"

"They've been married for a long time before she was in a coma. And a marriage that long is not without its troubles, but they always seem to work things out. One way or another," he assured him, sitting up.

Rhydian frowned. "I hope you're right."

Luxor put a hand on Rhydian's shoulder. "Your parents love each other very much, Rhydian. They will be all right.

This isn't even their worst fight." He gave him a comforting pat, then walked out of the room.

Rhydian was left alone with his thoughts. He worried for his parents and hoped they could work things out, as Luxor said. The last thing he wanted was for his parents to end their marriage because of his actions.

# CHAPTER 13

**B**lack crepe draped the great hall, as the Ausher house mourned. Roland had a portrait commissioned for the service based on Luxor's description. Rhianwen was the spitting image of Kezia, with fairer skin and Roland's eyes. Lilies and lavender surrounded the painting, and it was placed prominently to allow those in attendance to pay their respects. The eulogy was brief since they only just found out about her.

Roland had attempted to track his brother down and stop him in order to recover Rhianwen's body. They at least wanted something of her to bury. But Ozmir was far too cunning, and he stayed ahead of Roland at every turn.

Instead of working in his favor, the blood bond they shared only made it easier for his brother to get away. His guilt over Rhianwen's abduction as an infant still weighed on him. Had he insisted on being in the room when she was born, it would not have happened. And Kezia would not have been put in a coma. She would have been there, and they would have raised both their children together.

Those that attended the ceremony wore formal mourning attire. The women wore long black dresses and veils, while the men were in dark suits. The atmosphere was heavy with grief for the child that was lost. After the eulogy, there was a moment of silence to allow reflection.

During the memorial service, Roland, Kezia, and Rhydian's emotional states were deeply affected by the gravity of the occasion and the profound sense of loss they felt. Each feeling the other's grief through their bond only compounded things.

After their talk about her abuse of the tincture, Kezia had stopped using it. Her emotions were all over the place after a day off of it, but soon, she evened out. He had forgiven her for her outburst in front of Rhydian; he knew she did not mean what she said. She had an addiction, and they had blindsided her with it. Her reaction was expected, though it still hurt in the end. Taking a vase to the head did not help either.

Roland stood closest to Rhianwen's portrait, his face etched with sorrow and regret. His mind raced with thoughts of the life Rhianwen should have had and the moments they missed together. Tears welled up in his eyes, but he fought to maintain his composure. He needed to be strong for his wife and son. His heart ached with a mix of anger and guilt, especially towards his brother.

Kezia was more visibly emotional. She was the only one that noticed Rhianwen's pain and fear while in her coma, and she could do nothing to help her daughter. She sat quietly, her eyes red and swollen from crying. As she clung to his hand, Roland could only imagine where her mind drifted. He wondered if she blamed herself for not being stronger or for not calling out when the baby was being taken. Her grief was palpable, a raw and aching wound that not even mermaid tears could heal.

Roland looked over at Rhydian. The realization that he had a sister, only to lose her before they could meet, filled his eyes with immense sadness. He knew Rhydian mourned not just her death, but the life they could have shared—the secrets, the laughter, and the twin bond that were stolen from them. Roland understood the loss his son was feeling.

Roland struggled with his warring emotions as the service continued. He found himself wondering if there was something he could have done, some sign he missed that could have led to Rhianwen's rescue sooner. The thoughts weighed heavily on him and added to his emotional turmoil.

Following the indoor service, the family and guests proceeded to the garden for a lantern release ceremony. The family inscribed each lantern with a personal message to Rhianwen before they were lit and released into the evening sky. As they watched the lanterns float into the night, carrying their messages of love and apology, Roland held his wife and son close. He knew his brother had used a forbidden spell to take her body, and it destroyed her soul, but he would keep that knowledge to himself.

Roland looked down when he felt something brush up against his leg. It was Luxor in his feline form, his golden eyes glowing in the night. His discovery of Rhianwen's existence and his inability to save her was hard for him, or else he would not be in a tiny body purring at Roland's feet. He stayed close to Roland, offering silent support.

The service was brief. Roland did not want to stress Kezia out for longer than he had to. Though they had no body to bury, he knew the memorial was necessary to give them closure. After putting Kezia to bed, he retreated to his office. She had been on her feet for too long and needed rest.

He was not sure for how long he was alone in his office, but he perked up when the door opened and Rhydian wheeled Kezia in.

"Kezia? What are you doing up, love? I thought you were tired?" he asked, getting up to greet her.

"I was, but I didn't want to be alone," she replied in a somber tone. "I'm sorry if I'm disturbing your work."

"No, I was just going over some plans," he said.

"What sort of plans?" Rhydian asked.

Roland motioned for him to sit, then went back and sat at his desk. "I was going over the plans to have a circus come out and perform to celebrate your mother's awakening."

Kezia's face lit up with excitement. "Oh, my love, that sounds wonderful!"

"Yes, father, what a grand idea," Rhydian smiled.

"Thank you, but there's more to it," he said nervously. There was so much that he wanted to tell them, but it never seemed like a good time. And Vala was insistent.

Kezia's expression softened. "What is it, Roland?"

He could hear the worry in her voice. "Raesh is part of the circus I'm having come out."

Her eyes narrowed at him in anger. "Why would you do this?" she growled.

"I'm sorry, love, but it was the only way we could think of to get him," he started. "My brother has to be stopped, and capturing his dragon before he claims him is imperative."

"We? You're working with the Emori?" she hissed.

"Father, why?" Rhydian asked, disappointment in his tone.

"In order for my brother to become a god again, he needs all of his power."

"What does it matter if he kills that dragon and becomes a god again?" she spat.

"It matters because he will have to kill the two of you as well."

"What?" Rhydian gasped.

"The two of you share a small portion of his power and he will need it all. I promised my mother that I would stop him before that happens," he explained solemnly.

"Why you, Roland? She's a goddess. Why can't she stop him?"

"Because she can't while he's mortal, and it was part of the deal I made so that she would wake you."

"Oh," she said in surprise.

The room fell silent for a few moments.

"What is your plan, exactly? How will you catch and contain the dragon?" Rhydian asked, breaking the silence.

"I've caught and contained him once before. I can do it again."

"Then why involve the circus?" he inquired further.

"Because if he thinks it's a trap, he won't come. Though we plan to take his lover to lure him out here as a backup plan."

"Kidnapping someone? I don't know if I can be part of that," spoke Kezia. "It feels wrong."

"It is wrong. The one he cares for is an innocent, but no harm will come to him."

"I just hope you're making the right choice."

He caught her gaze and said, "When it comes to you, there is no right or wrong choice. I will always do what I have to do for you. You have given me life and a son, and will see this world drown if I ever lost you," he growled. "My brother will die before I let him near either of you."

They stared wide-eyed at him. He meant every word.

# Chapter 14

The path to the blacksmith's home was a narrow, winding trail carved into the rugged mountainside. The air was filled with a sense of foreboding, and the sky was overcast, creating eerie shadows on the rocky terrain. Dorjan was grateful it was not too far up the mountain.

As he trudged up the path, a chill ran down his spine. Out of the mist, a familiar figure appeared. Her head was full of wild curls, she had sickly pale skin, and a pair of brown eyes that were filled with a mix of amusement and rage. Her voice echoed with an unsettling, otherworldly quality.

"Hello, tiny grandpa," she grinned malevolently.

Dorjan stopped and grumbled at the sight of his dead granddaughter. He was tired of these kinds of spells. His mother was playing a game she was not going to win. He had no love or guilt towards anyone now. Nothing would stop him on his path of vengeance and justice.

"Though, I suppose I shouldn't call you that, seeing as though you're not tiny anymore," she giggled, following him when he moved past her.

"I don't have time for this," he muttered. "Go away."

She caught up to him, still smiling. "It's a long way up. I wouldn't want you to get lonely."

"I think I'll manage just fine on my own, thank you." He shook his head. He was actually talking to a spirit that was not actually there.

Rhianwen's soul was destroyed when he took her body. The ritual she read made sure of it. Not even a remnant of her soul lingered behind to irritate him for a while, like his sons had. She must have been ready to accept her fate.

"Well, what if I get lonely? Keeping me company is the least you could do, all things considered."

Dorjan growled in frustration as he continued up the mountain.

"You have no one to blame but yourself. You didn't have to steal me from my real family just so you could murder me. Now I've been left alone in limbo for all eternity," she sighed dramatically, then started laughing.

He found the apparition to be just as annoying as Rhianwen was in life. He was glad to be rid of the troublesome girl. Now, if he could only get rid of the bothersome illusion of her.

"Why won't you talk to me?" she pouted. "I'm so bored!"

Dorjan rolled his eyes as he kept going. He would have traveled through the shadows to get to the blacksmith, but there were no sufficient shadows for him to make use of. So, he had to walk… and deal with the nuisance at his side.

"Ugh, why are you being so cold? You used to give me whatever I wanted!" she whined. "Do you remember how it was back in London? How all the boys followed me around?"

He grumbled in response.

"Oh, how you hated it! But they were all so yummy!"

"Yes, and we had to move because of your ravenous appetite," he reminded her, then shook his head. It was not really her. She was just an illusion conjured from his memories of her.

"That was your decision. I was having fun and didn't see the problem."

Of course she did not. He had spoiled her, after all. He let her get away with multiple murders. The girl had no self-control.

She continued her tirade. "Not that it mattered where we lived. The boys still wanted me. And I wanted them," she grinned.

He continued to grumble as he walked.

"And I adored the little dress shop in London! But I loved the dressmaker's son so much more!" she laughed. "He was particularly flavorful and so eager to please me."

Again, Dorjan rolled his eyes as he sighed in exasperation.

"You know, you ought to be ashamed for using your familiars to trick me into killing you," she started. "All so you could steal my body. I hope you're enjoying the hunger pangs," she purred.

At that, Dorjan stopped and stared at her. There was a malevolent glee in her brown eyes. His brother's eyes. He growled in frustration, then continued on his path.

The girl went on blathering about one thing or another. He was not sure. He had stopped listening. Dorjan refused to let a false specter get into his head. Soon, the mist cleared up and an opening in the mountain's side appeared. Once he reached the entrance, the girl disappeared. She dissipated just as the mist had. Dorjan breathed a sigh of relief at being free of the irritant.

The cave entrance was hidden by thick vines and foliage, making it nearly invisible to the untrained eye. As Dorjan stepped inside, the air was cool and damp, with the faint smell of metal and fire lingering in the atmosphere. The path inside the cave was lit by glowing crystals embedded in the walls, casting a soft, ethereal light to guide the way.

The main chamber of the cave was vast, with a high ceiling that echoed the sounds of hammering and crackling fire. Shelves lined the walls, holding various tools, ingots of different metals, and magical artifacts likely collected over many years. The center of the chamber was dominated by a large forge, its flames dancing and casting flickering shadows around the room.

Near the forge sat the blacksmith's anvil, accompanied by a sturdy workbench laden with half-finished projects. Various hammers, tongs, and chisels hung from hooks on the wall, each one meticulously maintained and within easy reach. A large bellow sat beside the forge, ready to stoke the flames to the perfect temperature for forging.

On one side of the chamber, a cozy corner served as the blacksmith's living quarters. A simple cot with thick blankets was tucked against the wall, and a small table held a few personal items, including a worn leather journal and a collection of books on magic. A bubbling cauldron hung over a smaller hearth, filling the air with the comforting aroma of a hearty stew.

As Dorjan looked around, he noticed the cave had been imbued with subtle enchantments that enhanced the blacksmith's work. He saw spells woven into the walls to sharpen precision, guiding each hammer strike to flawless accuracy. He turned to see an enchantment was placed to maintain a consistent heat in the forge, ensuring the metal always remained pliable and uniform. And he could feel that the air itself was imbued with a charm to ward off fatigue, granting the blacksmith endurance far beyond mortal limits. His fingers ran over the runes etched into the walls that pulsed with a faint, otherworldly glow, providing protection and amplifying the magical properties of the forge. The air hummed with latent energy, making it clear that this was a place where ordinary metal could be transformed into extraordinary weapons and artifacts.

The blacksmith's home was just as Dorjan expected and more. A deep, resonating voice rumbled with laughter from behind Dorjan. He turned to see who he assumed was the blacksmith, an imposing figure who commanded attention the moment he stepped into view. Standing over six feet tall, his broad shoulders and muscular build were a testament to years of hard labor and possible battles. His skin was weathered from exposure to the elements, and his arms were covered in intricate tattoos that told a story of what Dorjan believed to be a Viking heritage.

His face was framed by a thick mane of fair hair, streaked with silver, and a full beard that reached his chest. He had piercing blue eyes that were like icy fjords, sharp and unwavering, hinting at the wisdom and strength he possessed. Despite his intimidating appearance, there was a sense of calm and focus about him that spoke to his mastery of both metal and magic.

Dorjan looked him up and down to see he was dressed in sturdy leather and furs and moved with the grace of a seasoned warrior. Around his neck, he wore a pendant shaped like a hammer, a symbol of his trade and a nod to the Norse god, Thor. The calloused hands that wielded hammers and tongs with precision were also capable of crafting intricate runes and enchantments into his work.

The heat from the forge cast a warm glow on the blacksmith's rugged features, highlighting the scars and lines that marked a life well-lived. His voice, deep and resonant, carried a hint of his native tongue, adding to the air of mystery and power that surrounded him.

"I can see that you appreciate my home," he said as he brought in heavy logs. "May I ask why you have chosen to invade it? Choose your answer wisely, stranger," he warned, his muscles suddenly taut. Like he was getting ready to strike at any moment.

Dorjan straightened his back and cleared his throat. "I am the god Ozmir, and I am Fallen."

The blacksmith dropped his pile of logs when Dorjan reached into the bag he was carrying and put his hand on the axe hanging from the belt at his side. The sound of the wood clattering to the cavern floor echoed throughout the space. Dorjan quickly put his hands up in surrender, holding his scale in one hand.

"I mean you no harm. I've simply come with a request for your services."

Slowly, the larger man moved his hand away from his weapon, staring at the scale in Dorjan's hand with wonder and awe. "Where did you get that?"

"It was mine before I fell. I had it hidden on earth for a very long time," Dorjan explained.

He handed the scale over to the eager blacksmith, who marveled at every detail of it, turning it over in his hands repeatedly, making sure he did not miss anything.

"It's beautiful," he murmured. "I must have it."

"I'm afraid I still have need of it," Dorjan admitted.

"I'll trade you whatever you want for it, but I must have it for my collection," he insisted, finally looking back up at Dorjan. His voice sounded desperate and full of greed.

"I assure you," Dorjan started, taking the scale back from the reluctant blacksmith, "you have nothing I could possibly want more than what I need this for."

The blacksmith narrowed his eyes at him. "What need of you with the scale of a dragon god?"

"That is my business, but know that you will be paid handsomely for your services."

He made a clicking sound with his tongue, his lip curling up. "I have no need of your coin," he said, moving to pick up the logs he had dropped. Once he had them all gathered back up in his arms, he carried them over to his forge. "How did you come to know of me?"

"I heard rumors of your forge and the weapons that come from it," Dorjan said, placing the scale back into his bag and following him. "What should I call you, by the way? No one seemed to know what exactly your name was."

He smiled at that. "I have had many names over the centuries, but you may call me Ulfberht."

"Very well, Ulfberht it is."

Ulfberht sat down on a stool behind his anvil, the wood creaking under his weight. "What will you have me craft for you?"

"I have need of a sword made out of my scale," Dorjan said. "It needs to be strong and capable of killing a god and destroying souls."

Ulfberht laughed. "A sword like that will be... expensive to make."

Dorjan furrowed his brow. "I thought you had no need of my coin?"

"Oh, I don't. I deal in souls and memories," he explained. "And I will be needing both from you with a blood oath."

Dorjan smiled broadly. "Whose soul and what memory?"

"The spell for such a sword will need powerful binding magic," he started. "I'm going to need the memory of the one person you ever loved... and your soul upon your death."

This time Dorjan sneered at Ulfberht. "At my death, you may have my soul, but I love no one."

He made another clicking sound with his tongue as he shook his head. "I don't believe that. You're on a path of vengeance from the sound of things. Whether you want to admit it or not, you loved someone at some point in your life. If not, why go through all this trouble for a weapon that can kill a god and destroy souls?"

"Again, that is my business. Can you make the sword, or not?" he asked impatiently.

Ulfberht smirked. "I can make it, but I will still need that memory." He stood, towering over Dorjan. "There is no need to tell me. The memory will come once I begin the extraction."

Dorjan glared up at Ulfberht, defiance in his eyes. "Fine, take the memory if you can find it. I have no need for such sentiments."

Ulfberht placed his large hands on Dorjan's shoulders. Dorjan felt small and vulnerable under their weight, and he did not like the look in Ulfberht's eyes. As if he was up to no good.

"Close your eyes and clear your mind. The memory will come," Ulfberht murmured.

Dorjan did as instructed and closed his eyes, trying to quiet the rage swirling in his mind. He felt Ulfberht remove one hand from his shoulder and place it on his head. A warm feeling passed through Dorjan as Ulfberht started a chant in an ancient tongue, the words resonating with the magic that filled the cave. The air crackled with energy as Ulfberht gripped Dorjan's head.

"Focus on the feeling of love, even if you think you haven't experienced it. Let the magic guide you," he said softly.

Dorjan's body tensed as he felt a strange sensation, like a gentle pull at the core of his mind. Slowly, memories surfaced—ones he had buried deep within himself. The image of his brother, Zaven, came into focus. He remembered the bond they shared, the laughter, the support, and the love that had once filled his heart. Tears streamed down his face as the memories came flooding back.

"The heart remembers what the mind forgets," Ulfberht spoke.

Ulfberht's hold on Dorjan's head tightened more, and with a final incantation, he drew the memories out completely. Dorjan opened his eyes and fell to his knees, the weight of the loss still heavy in his heart. He took them all. All the love he had for his brother was gone, leaving only the hate and betrayal behind.

With his hands in tight fists at his sides, Dorjan got back on his feet. "Was that all you needed?" he asked through gritted teeth.

"No, there is more," Ulfberht started. "We must make a blood pact for your soul to complete the transaction."

Dorjan narrowed his eyes. "Why do you need such things?"

"Memories and souls are powerful magic that I use in forging my items and for making trades with others that practice the arts as I do."

Dorjan smiled knowingly. He would soon have his immortality back. His soul was safe, no matter the deal. "Let's just get this over with."

Ulfberht also smiled, pulling a hunting knife from a sheath on his belt. He took hold of Dorjan's left hand and faced it palm up before slicing it open. He did the same with his left hand, then clasped their hands together, mingling their blood. "Should you renege on this pact, the sword I forge will turn against you in battle."

Before Dorjan could speak again, Ulfberht began another incantation. This one sounded just as ancient as the last. A bright white light emanated from their joined hands, turning from a burst to wispy strands of light that coiled around their wrists and joined them. Dorjan noted it was similar to the bond formed with familiars.

At the end of the incantation, the light dispersed in a violent flash, temporarily blinding Dorjan. Ulfberht had released his hand, and Dorjan heard him walk away. The same creaking sound from his work stool seemed that much louder without his sight. When he could see again,

Dorjan noticed that his bag had been cut from him, and Ulfberht was holding the scale again.

"Come back in one week's time," Ulfberht said without looking at him. "Your sword will be ready then."

"It had better be," Dorjan growled. "I don't make blood pacts lightly. Betray me at your own peril, Ulfberht."

Again, Ulfberht laughed. It was another deep rumble that filled the cavern. "You have my word that a sword to kill a god and destroy souls will be crafted from this scale. It will be my finest work."

"Then I will leave you to it."

With his memories taken and the blood pact made, Dorjan turned to leave the cave. Once outside, he fully expected to see the illusion of his granddaughter again, but he found himself traveling down the mountainside blissfully alone.

# CHAPTER 15

The circus wrapped up their tour early to prepare for the private performance at the Ausher mansion in Wales. They returned to their home base, and Raesh helped Aiden formulate a plan of escape should things go wrong. They would leave in a little over a week, so Raesh took a few days to go over what he wanted to ask Korlue before going to see him.

The uncertainty of what he wanted frustrated him. What if Korlue did not want the same things? Raesh found himself wondering if he wanted to settle at all. Was he ready?

"Andrew? What are you doing back so soon? Come to get your fix?" Korlue asked, grinning deceptively as he reclined suggestively across the bed in an all too revealing robe.

"Not now, Korlue," he said flatly. "I have something I wish to discuss with you, and I am in no mood for games." He crossed the room to meet the other man.

"And what are you in the mood for?" he purred, sitting up only to have to crane his neck to look up at the taller man. He walked his thin fingers up the length of Raesh's chest, receiving a feral growl. "You know, you'd make a decent Host and earn a great deal of money—"

Raesh snarled furiously and grabbed Korlue, pinning to the bed with a firm grip on his throat. Korlue chuckled nervously at the rage in Raesh's eyes. They had been getting into role playing recently, but it was not a good time. Raesh had a lot on his mind, and he wanted to talk.

"All right, Andy, you can let me go now. What has you so riled up?"

Raesh took a calming breath, then released Korlue. He watched as Korlue rubbed his neck, a worried look in his crystal blue eyes. "I apologize for my outburst," he said, sitting next to him with his head held down.

Korlue rested his hand on Raesh's leg, dipping his head to regain eye contact with him. "What is it?" he asked softly.

Raesh gently squeezed Korlue's hand and gave him a light kiss on the lips. "The circus has been summoned to perform at the Ausher mansion for a private show in Wales." He decided to wait to talk about Korlue leaving his Host life behind to be with him full time.

Korlue's eyes lit up. "As in the Ausher Apothecary, Ausher?"

Raesh only nodded.

"That's pretty far away, but you'll come back in a couple of weeks or so."

"That is not what is bothering me." Not all of it, anyway.

"Then what is? Talk to me," Korlue pleaded lightly.

"I do not believe that I will be welcomed there again."

"Again? Andrew, what happened?"

Raesh took another calming breath before speaking again. "I tried to kill his wife," he said after a moment. "But she was pregnant, so I hesitated."

The information stunned Korlue into a brief silence. Raesh studied his face for any sign of disgust or fear, but Korlue's expression remained one of worry.

"Does Ausher know you're with the circus? Of course he does. Your face is all over the flyers!" he rambled off before Raesh could respond. "Maybe you shouldn't go. This could go badly."

"We have an escape plan should that be the case, but I am Sacha's partner, and she cannot do the show with anyone else," he explained.

"What if he has you arrested?"

"He would do far worse than have me arrested. My time training his wife before they wed was… unpleasant for her," he said solemnly. "I have a lot to atone for, and he will want his pound of flesh."

"But you're an immortal dragon. He can't really hurt you," Korlue tried.

Raesh paused, uncertain he wanted to tell Korlue of his time with Roland Ausher. "He is a god, he can kill me… probably," he said with a half-hearted smirk. "He will certainly try."

"Oh, then you're definitely not going," Korlue insisted, getting up to stand in front of Raesh, his hands firmly on his hips. "You'd be crazy to go."

Raesh smiled and looked up at his lover. "If I do not go, we do not get paid. If I do not get paid, I cannot pay for your upkeep."

Korlue gently took Raesh's face into his small hands, and Raesh felt the warm, electric buzz of his touch.

"I can start taking guests again," he offered.

Raesh frowned at that. "No," he growled out, taking Korlue by the waist and pulling him close. "You are mine."

"And you are mine. I don't want anything to happen to you," he murmured, his lips lightly brushing his.

"I know, but the circus is my family. I do not know what Ausher's intentions are, and I do not want them without my protection."

When Raesh went to kiss him, Korlue pulled away.

"Don't try to distract me. I'm your family, too," he scowled.

Raesh pulled him into his lap, getting a surprised yelp from him. "We leave in four days. You have me until then." Before Korlue could protest, Raesh crushed his lips to his and laid him down. He left a trail of kisses along Korlue's jaw and down his neck. "I will come back to you," he whispered, then sank his fangs into his throat.

Korlue gasped, then let out a moan.

Raesh pulled back once he had his fill, and with hooded eyes he asked, "May I have you now?" his voice heavy with lust.

Korlue nodded slowly, a luster of need in his eyes.

Raesh stood to undress himself, and Korlue sat up.

"Here," Korlue said. "Let me do it." His nimble fingers made quick work of the buttons on Raesh's shirt.

Raesh watched as Korlue slid his hands up and down his chest and over his shoulders, sliding the shirt off of him. Practiced hands undid his trousers, his eyes never leaving his. Raesh stepped out of his trousers, which left only his underwear. Korlue went to work undoing those as well, freeing Raesh from his linen confines as he dropped to his knees.

His cock rose up with its thick, hard shaft. Korlue tipped his head back to look Raesh in the eyes again.

"I want to properly earn my keep," he smiled.

Raesh groaned when Korlue's warm breath touched him. He threaded his fingers through Korlue's fine hair and returned his smile. "Then earn it." His free hand wrapped around the base of his shaft. "Take me into your mouth, Korlue."

"Yes, sir." He licked his lips before he took the smooth, mushroom tip between his lips, closing them around the base of the head and sucking lightly before he released it. "Is this to your liking?"

Raesh's fingers made a fist in Korlue's hair, urging him to take him back into his mouth. "Yes," he moaned. "Make me come with your mouth."

Korlue looked up at Raesh as he stroked his shaft with his tongue before taking him into his mouth again. Raesh watched Korlue's face, and the sight of his cock between Korlue's lips and the warmth of his mouth further excited him. He was getting harder.

"Take more of me," Raesh murmured, thrusting forward. "Yes, like that. Gods, your mouth feels like heaven."

Korlue groaned around his cock, the vibrations making Raesh impossibly harder. He looked down and saw Korlue's bobbing erection leaking as he continued to service him.

"Touch yourself for me," he commanded as he thrusted gently in and out of Korlue's sinful mouth.

As ordered, Korlue took hold of his own erection while he sucked Raesh off.

"Harder. Suck harder," he said, his voice barely above a growl. "Take as much of me in as you are able. Yes, very good. Just like that." He was sliding in and out of his mouth, and then, with no warning, he wrenched himself free. He did not want his release just yet.

Before Korlue could do anything more than whimper his discontent, Raesh had him flat on his back on the bed. Raesh climbed on top of him and kissed him fiercely. He blazed a trail of kisses down Korlue's neck, moving to his chest. His tongue found Korlue's erect nipple and massaged it before his lips wrapped around it. Korlue gasped and arched into Raesh's mouth when he bit down on his nipple and pinched the other between his calloused fingers.

Raesh moved from his chest down to the flat of his stomach, lingering at his navel before going below his waist. He took hold of Korlue's member and ran his tongue up the underside of it, then took him into his mouth. He sucked him hard with a steady rhythm, pulling him closer by his hips to take more of him in.

When Korlue cried out his release, Raesh held on to him, refusing to let go until he calmed down.

"Did I do something wrong?" Korlue asked, panting from his release.

"No," Raesh replied, wiping the corner of his mouth. "I only wanted you to come first." He moved up and kissed him reassuringly.

"Your mouth is amazing!" he sighed. "What about you?"

"Oh, I intend to have my pleasures," he grinned, hovering over him. "Are you ready for me?"

"Always," he smiled ruefully.

Raesh positioned the head of his cock at Korlue's rear, then entered him slowly. They both grunted at how tight of a fit it was. He needed a moment to adjust to the feeling. He always filled him so completely. Once he was ready, he pumped in and out of Korlue, reveling in his warmth.

He maintained a steady pace until he felt himself getting close to climax. He could tell Korlue was almost there again, so he leaned forward and kissed him. "Come for me," he whispered in his ear, his voice deep and inviting.

When Raesh sank his fangs into him again, Korlue shook as he came a second time, clawing the hard muscles in Raesh's back. Raesh took no blood from him this time, only wanting to feel him shudder beneath him and mark him as his. The simple act of claiming his lover sent him over the edge, and he released all that he had into him.

Once they both calmed, Raesh pulled out of him and laid beside him.

"Did you just mark me?" he asked, feeling the bite, but not the draw of his blood.

"I did," he admitted.

"Is that normal for dragons?"

"I do not know, but it is normal for wolves," he explained. "I have a werewolf's bite, and occasionally transform, remember?"

"Right, I forgot. Why did you do it?"

Raesh took a moment before answering. "I believe you to be my mate. I want no one else."

"Oh," Korlue replied, averting his eyes.

Raesh lifted Korlue's chin to look at him. "Does knowing this displease you?"

"What?" he asked in surprise. "No, of course not."

"Then what is wrong?"

"I just never thought anyone would want me as a mate," he muttered. "It's a little unnerving."

"I understand," he said, releasing his chin.

Korlue ran his hands up and down Raesh's chest, silence filling the room briefly. "Why me?" he asked after a few moments.

"Because no one else matters to me as you do," he replied.

Korlue chuckled. "That's a funny way of saying it, but I love you, too," he said, nuzzling him.

Raesh went stiff for a moment, then gently pushed Korlue away to look him in the eyes again. "Do you mean that?"

"Didn't you?" he smiled.

"Yes."

"Then it's settled. I am your mate, and you are mine."

Raesh pulled Korlue back to him in a tight embrace and gave him a lingering kiss. Korlue, in turn, let his hand trail down the front of him.

Raesh was hard again the moment Korlue touched him, and he rolled on top of him. "I am going to fuck you until this entire building can hear you scream my name," he growled. He kissed him again before he could respond.

They made love for hours, and the sun was rising by the time Raesh had reached his limit. Before he fell into a well-deserved slumber, he got out of bed to retrieve a small box from the pocket of his previously discarded coat.

Korlue sat up tiredly, his curiosity getting the better of him.

"I brought something for you." He presented Korlue with the box and watched as he gleefully tore through the wrapping and opened it.

His eyes lit up at the sight of what was inside. Raesh had spent hours scrubbing it clean, making sure to remove any trace of the former owner's blood. It was the grounding stone necklace Raesh had taken from another lightning elemental that the Emori had sent to drug him. He had killed the elemental, of course. Now the obsidian stone gleamed with the same intensity as Korlue's eyes when he looked at it.

"Andy, this looks expensive!" He was giddy when Raesh went to put it on him.

He would not tell him where the necklace came from. "You need not worry about such things," he said, lying back down.

"Well, I love it. Thank you." He planted a soft kiss on Raesh's cheek, then laid down beside him. "I was wondering..."

"Hm?" Raesh asked with a tired groan.

"Since I only have you for three more days now, I thought we could go to the masquerade ball being held in a couple of days. I was going to take my bodyguard, but now that I have you..."

Raesh groaned disapprovingly, his eyes shut.

"Please, I'd really like to go. Especially with my mate."

He opened his eyes halfway. Korlue was using his feelings for him against him. He had to admit, it was working. "Fine," he grumbled, pulling Korlue against him. "Just go to sleep now."

Korlue yawned. "Yes, my mate," he grinned against Raesh's chest.

Raesh smiled as he drifted off to sleep. He officially had a mate now. He would talk to him about moving in with him when he was better rested.

# CHAPTER 16

R oland stood at the window, looking into the
night. The moonlight cast a silver glow on his
stern features. He had a lot on his mind that
evening, most of it was his worry over Kezia. She did not
agree with what he wanted to do, but gave her support
anyway. Still, kidnapping an innocent man did not sit
right with him.

He turned to the door when he heard it open, and
Luxor brought an elderly monk, along with a few others,
into his office.

"Thank you for coming," Roland said, offering seats.
"We need to make changes to the plans." He sat down
behind his desk.

The elderly monk that called himself Brother Thane nodded, taking a seat on the other side of the desk. "I understand that you have some concerns about certain parts?"

"Yes, we would rather not have the circus come out. That would be too many innocent people fighting to help Raesh."

"Of course, the circus is a liability. They are a troop of reformed killers and thieves. It's best not to risk them being here to help the dragon," Thane said. "Their ringleader is a former agent of ours, and he will do whatever he can to protect him."

"Wait, if he was one of you, why is he protecting him?" asked Luxor.

"He left the order some time ago to run his father's circus. He didn't agree with our methods of dealing with Lyr'kin," Thane explained.

"That would have been nice to know before we invited the lot out here," Roland growled. "You could have put my family in danger."

"You needn't worry about them. I have already sent a message to our agents in America to cancel the performance."

"Then how do we get Raesh out here?" Luxor questioned. "He's dangerous and you don't have the best track record of keeping him contained."

"Our agents are in place to take both Raesh and his lover in two days' time. They will be brought here for containment," said Thane.

"Why are we still kidnapping his lover?" asked Roland.

"Korlue is vital to the plan. He will ensure that the dragon stays contained until your brother is dealt with."

"What's to stop Raesh from taking his lover back from you?" asked Luxor. "How do you plan to get them here safely?"

Roland looked over at the agitated feline. He wanted no part in this either, but his bond with Roland demanded otherwise. Though Roland would never enforce it. His family was as much a priority to Luxor as it was to him.

A young monk stood and spoke. "We have enchanted iron restraints for the dragon, blessed by the goddess. They should hold him long enough for us to bring him here."

Roland's jaw tightened at the mention of his mother. "All right. And what about this Korlue?"

Thane smiled slightly. "Korlue will be kept separate from the dragon. We have a special sedative to keep them both unconscious for the trip out here."

The group spent the next hour meticulously going over every detail of their plans to contain Raesh and lure Ozmir out to his death. Roland's mind raced with the possibilities and the risks, but he knew that this was their best shot of succeeding.

As the meeting concluded, Thane placed a hand on Roland's shoulder as he stood beside him. "Trust in the goddess, Zaven. We will succeed."

Roland's gaze hardened. "I will never trust her, but I can learn to trust you. For now, that's enough."

"For Vala," the Emori spoke, their voices filled with determination.

With the plan set, Roland and the Emori prepared for the coming battle, knowing that the fate of the mission—and perhaps much more—hung in the balance.

After the Emori left, Roland and Luxor examined their own plans, anticipating problems and Roland's possible death.

"I need you and Nox to make sure my family stays safe if I can't kill Ozmir."

"Perhaps you should talk with them about this," said Luxor.

Roland shook his head. "No, I don't want them involved any more than they are."

"Fine," Luxor sighed in exasperation. "What will you have me do?"

"Take them to the safe house we set up in London," he said. "Keep them hidden from Ozmir for as long as you can."

"And what are we to do about feeding their lust?"

"Ariel has already seen to that, and Rhydian will have Dorian with him," Roland explained.

"Do you really think it'll come to that? You've fought him once before and won."

"I didn't know he was my brother then. He was scared, and not willing to fight me." Despite the bad blood between them, he was still his brother, and killing him did not feel right. He wished he could talk with Ozmir to stop all this, but Roland had made a promise to a goddess. One he could not break.

"Zaven?" Luxor called softly.

"I'm all right, Lux. Just doing a bit of thinking."

"I'm sorry, Zaven. For all of this. I should've realized something was wrong with the midwife sooner. I could have spared you of this."

Roland smiled wryly at him. "There's no way you could have known. She fooled us all, so don't beat yourself up over it."

"Then I ask that you take your own advice."

"Yes, father," Roland chuckled, getting up to leave.

Luxor narrowed his eyes, following him. "And don't call me that. It's weird," he said, shutting the door behind them.

"Good night, Lux," Roland waved as he went down the hall in the opposite direction.

"Good night, Zaven," he replied.

Roland went up the stairs and straight to the master bedroom on the third floor. It was late. He knew Kezia would be asleep by now. He quietly opened the door and stood there briefly, admiring his love as she slept with her back to the door. A sigh escaped him. He really would do anything to make sure she was happy and safe. Leaving her was going to break both their hearts.

# CHAPTER 17

*H*e sat brooding. *Flickering torchlight adorned his dark, ethereal throne room, casting eerie shadows on the ancient stone walls. At the center of the room stood a large viewing orb, its surface swirling with mist and images of the mortal realm.*

*Ozmir's eyes, filled with a mixture of frustration and longing, were fixed on the orb. Through the enchanted surface, he watched his twin, who roamed freely in the mortal realm with his mortal wife. Zaven's life contrasted sharply with Ozmir's existence in the underworld; Zaven's life was filled with light and love, while Ozmir's was filled with gloom and isolation.*

*As Ozmir observed Zaven and his mortal, a pang of jealousy gnawed at his heart. He remembered the days when he and Zaven were inseparable, their bond forged in the fires of eternity. They had cared for the souls of the drowned side by side, always together. But fate had torn them apart, and now Zaven had found solace in the arms of a mortal woman, leaving Ozmir to dwell alone in the shadows. Facing the ridicule and wrath of their family on his own.*

*The viewing orb showed him scenes of Zaven's daily life with his wife. They walked hand in hand through sunlit meadows, shared laughter over meals, and found joy in each other's presence. Each moment of happiness they experienced felt like a knife in Ozmir's heart, a reminder of the life he once had and the brother he had lost.*

*His irritation only grew with each passing scene. He resented Zaven for moving on, for finding happiness without him. He resented the woman for taking his brother's love and attention. But beneath the anger, there was an ache of longing, a desire to be part of his brother's world once more.*

*Ozmir clenched his fists, his nails digging into his palms. "How can he forget our bond so easily?" he muttered, his voice echoing through the empty throne room. "How can he find happiness in the arms of a mortal while I languish here, alone?"*

*Though he had Azier and SeVhon, it was not the same. They were usually off together when they were not quieting rebellious souls and patrolling the realms. Despite his frustration, Ozmir could not tear his gaze away from the orb. He was drawn to the love and warmth that radiated from Zaven and his woman. The more he watched, the more he realized he hated mortals all the more.*

*Yet, he kept watching. He watched as his brother made love to his mortal. The deep intimacy between them was unlike anything he had ever seen. The way her body gave in to his brother's will, the sounds she made. It was all so infuriating. He did not understand the appeal. It disgusted him. How could his brother be with a mortal like that?*

*With a wave of his hand, the image disappeared from the orb. Ozmir sat there fuming. Did his brother really abandon him for the flesh of a mortal woman?*

Dorjan sneered at the memory. He did not understand why it even came up, but he lost himself in it. And then, he felt the unfortunately familiar lust rise within him. He needed to hunt now. His lip curled up at the thought. He hated that he needed to feed his unwanted desires to sustain his body. It was a baser instinct that he could never understand the need for other than for procreation. He never enjoyed the act, especially with mortals. Filthy creatures that they were.

The streets of New Orleans were alive with the sounds of jazz, laughter, and whispered secrets. Dorjan prowled the shadowy streets with predatory intentions, his eyes gleaming with a malevolent glint. The city's nightlife was his hunting ground, and despite his disdain for his needs, he reveled in the thrill of the hunt. Disguised in his mortal form, his charisma and charm drew people to him like moths to a flame. The music of a nearby jazz club drifted through the air, mingling with the scent of magnolia blossoms and the distant rumble of horse-drawn carriages.

As Dorjan made his way through the crowded streets towards the club, he scanned the faces of those around him, seeking the perfect target. His gaze fell upon a young woman standing alone, her expression wistful as she listened to the music. She was beautiful, with dark curls cascading over her shoulders and a dress that shimmered in the moonlight. Her aura radiated a sweetness that was irresistible to his demon.

With a practiced smile, Dorjan approached her, his voice smooth and inviting. "Good evening, miss. May I have the pleasure of your company for a dance?"

His presence was magnetic, and the woman found herself drawn to him, unable to resist the allure of his jewel green eyes.

She nodded, and Dorjan led her to the dance floor of the club, where the band played a soulful melody. They moved together in perfect harmony; the music wrapped around them like a spell. As they danced, Dorjan whispered sweet words into her ear, weaving a web of enchantment that left her captivated. As he had done with the women who bore his children, and those who had fallen victim to his lust recently.

Beneath his charming exterior, Dorjan's true nature stirred. He could feel the energy of the woman pulsing through her, a tantalizing source of life force that he craved. The closer they danced, the stronger his hunger grew. He tightened his grip on her waist, drawing her closer, his breath warm against her neck.

As the dance drew to a close, Dorjan leaned in, his lips brushing against the woman's ear. "Come with me," he whispered, his voice a seductive promise.

She nodded, her eyes glazed with infatuation, and allowed him to lead her out of the club and into the quiet alleyway beyond.

He pressed her against the wall, his eyes boring into hers. His lips lightly brushed against hers in a sweeping motion as his hands traveled along her body. He kissed her fiercely, snaking one of his hands under her dress. He grinned against her lips when there was a sharp intake of air from her. His long, nimble fingers had found their prize. She was soaking wet for him.

Dorjan found he wanted to taste her. He wanted to know if she was as sweet as she smelled. His demon demanded it. He slid down her body and got down on his knees. He hiked up her dress, exposing her to the warm night air, and roughly pulled her forward by her hips. His eyes never left hers as he spread her legs apart.

He let out a groan as the smell of her sweet scent hit him. The rapid rise and fall of her breasts and her ragged breathing urged him on. He ran his tongue across her slit from the base to her clit, making her shudder when he enveloped the bundle of nerves with his lips. He used his fingers to spread her swollen folds apart, then he stuck his tongue inside of her. She was sweet indeed.

She sighed with the contact, a soft moan escaping her lips. He held her up by the hips as he devoured her, his tongue swirling and darting in and out of her. He nipped at and tongue fucked her until she came undone in his mouth. The music was loud enough to drown out her cry of satisfaction, which he was grateful for. He did not want them to be interrupted.

He got back to his feet, licking her juices from his lips. "Non, non, Cherie. You must be silent, or someone will come looking for you," he murmured into her ear as he pressed himself against her. His erection was straining against his trousers, begging for release. He needed to be as deep inside of her as he could get.

She giggled, covering her mouth with her hands. He undid the front of his trousers, then lifted her above the instrument of his demonic need. She arched her back as he plunged into the depths of her desire.

His thrusts came hard but were steady. Her legs wrapped around his waist, pulling him in deeper. As much as he hated to admit it, he was enjoying himself. But he just brushed it off as a byproduct of his incubus nature. There was no genuine feeling for him. It was just something he needed to do.

He grunted as he pumped into her faster; he was getting close to his own release. Soon, he felt the warmth of her life force flowing into him. It was such an odd sensation, something akin to being filled with joy and life itself. He could not really describe it, but it made him feel powerful. And it tingled a little. When the realization of what was happening hit her, he covered her mouth to silence her scream.

His release was hard and fast, and he shot his load into her as he drained her essence. Her hands fell to her sides as her skin shrunk tightly around her bones. Once he was done with her, he pulled out of her and let her fall to the ground. He looked down at the ashen gray husk covered in a now ill-fitting red dress, and buttoned up his trousers, walking away with a devilish smile on his satisfied face.

While he did not enjoy the act of mating, the end result was now much more pleasant than it was before he took over his granddaughter's body. He left the alley feeling an otherworldly buzz. High from his kill and her life-sustaining energy.

# CHAPTER 18

When they arrived at the mansion of a wealthy local, the festivities were already underway. The main entrance was a breathtaking sight, even by Raesh's high standards. Every aspect was designed to impress and enchant every guest who stepped through it. He and Korlue were no exception.

The entrance hall featured gleaming marble floors, polished to a mirror-like finish. The intricate patterns in the marble added a touch of sophistication and grandeur. There were high, vaulted ceilings adorned with elaborate frescoes depicting scenes of myth and legend. Rich, dark wood formed the double doors leading into the ballroom; these doors featured intricate carvings of floral motifs and gilded accents. Artisans crafted elegant, scroll-shaped handles from polished gold. They gleamed in the soft light.

On either side of the entrance were large, ornate vases overflowing with fresh flowers in vibrant colors. Garlands of greenery and flowers gracefully adorned the doorframe. Above the entrance was a crystal chandelier that cast a warm, inviting glow. The light reflected off the crystals and created a dazzling display of light and shadow. Along the walls were candlelit sconces that provided additional soft lighting, their flickering flames added to the romantic ambiance.

A plush red carpet led from the entrance hall into the ballroom to guide guests towards the heart of the festivities. The carpet was soft underfoot and added to the sense of luxury.

They stepped into the ballroom where the air was thick with jasmine and the sound of a lively jazz band filled the room. Rich velvet drapes in deep burgundy and gold lined the walls, and many crystal chandeliers emitted a warm, flickering light over the scene. The dance floor itself was made of polished hardwood, gleaming under the soft light of the chandeliers. It was expansive, providing ample space for guests to move freely and expressively.

The guests, dressed in elaborate costumes, glided across the floor. Women wore opulent gowns with intricate beadwork and lace, their faces hidden behind ornate masks adorned with feathers and jewels. Men were equally resplendent in tailored suits and capes with matching masks.

Raesh also wore a black tailored suit with an emerald silk waistcoat. His mask was a simple yet elegant black half-mask, with a subtle gold filigree. Korlue was striking in his flowing, emerald gown that shimmered under the candlelight. He wore a delicate gold and green mask, decorated with complex patterns and tiny gemstones that caught the light with every movement. While Raesh's hair was in its usual neat braid, Korlue's was perfectly coiffed in an updo.

Raesh had briefly wondered why Korlue chose to wear a gown and present himself as female, but he remembered the taboo of their relationship, and Korlue was often mistaken for a woman. Even if he wore a suit, Raesh would have been proud to have him on his arm for the evening.

Korlue practically vibrated with excitement once they were inside. Elegant silverware and fine China decorated the tables, and the waitstaff, dressed in crisp uniforms, moved gracefully through the crowd. They kept every guest's glass full and their plates replenished. The food consisted of fresh oysters topped with a rich mixture of butter, parsley, and breadcrumbs, then baked to perfection. There were succulent shrimp served with a tangy, creamy remoulade sauce, garnished with fresh herbs, and a flavorful dish of crawfish smothered in a decadent, spicy sauce, served over a bed of fluffy white rice.

There were tender beef fillets wrapped in puff pastries with a layer of pâté and duxelles, baked until golden brown. A blend of Creole spices seasoned a hearty mix of rice, sausage, chicken, and shrimp. And there were light, airy pastries dusted with powdered sugar, offering a sweet finish to the meal.

The drinks were equally tempting. Raesh selected a cocktail made with rye whiskey, absinthe, a sugar cube, and Peychaud's bitters served in an old-fashioned glass. Korlue chose a fruity, rum-based cocktail with passion fruit juice, lime juice, and grenadine served in a tall glass with a cherry and orange slice garnish.

The careful consideration of every detail created an overall effect of timeless elegance and enchantment for a magical and unforgettable evening. The combination of jazz and classical music created a dynamic and captivating soundscape.

Raesh did his best to enjoy himself, but he had a nagging suspicion that something was wrong. He felt the gentle touch of Korlue's hand on his as he scanned the room, observing all the guests. He turned to his lover—his mate—to see a worried look in his cornflower blue eyes.

"What's wrong?" he asked.

He smiled warmly at him. "It is nothing. I am just not used to these types of functions any longer."

"Are you sure? Are people staring at us?" he wondered, looking around frantically.

Raesh gently squeezed his hand and smiled at him again. "If they are staring, it is only because you look magnificent. You're the most beautiful one here."

Korlue blushed at that. "You're just saying that."

"Yes, but I mean every word."

"You are too kind, sir," he beamed. Suddenly, he perked up. "Ooh, I love this song! Let's dance!"

This time Raesh blushed. "No, it has been too long since I have—"

Korlue had hopped out of his seat and jerked Raesh out of his with strength Raesh did not know Korlue had, and dragged him to the dance floor. After a few awkward moments and stiff movements, Raesh found his rhythm. The music playing was a smooth, sultry blues piece that eventually transitioned into a waltz. A dance Raesh was more familiar with. As they danced, the waitstaff brought them glasses of champagne, and Raesh thought about what he wanted to ask Korlue.

"You always look so pensive when you're thinking," Korlue giggled. "What's on your mind now?"

"You, of course," Raesh replied, pulling him close.

"Oh really? Am I doing naughty things to you in that handsome head of yours?"

Again, Raesh blushed.

"Andrew! There are people around," he fussed quietly.

Raesh chuckled. "I cannot help it. Especially when you are this close."

"You are absolutely shameless!" he laughed.

Korlue's laughter was like music to him. "Move in with me," he said after a moment.

Korlue blinked wildly at him. "But what of the Club?"

"What of it? You are no longer working," Raesh reminded him.

"But I have so much stuff."

"And I do not. There is plenty of room for you," he retorted.

"All right, but what will I do while you're away with the circus?" Korlue questioned.

"I will be retiring soon. Sacha has gotten older and is not as able to keep up with me. And I do not wish to train a replacement for her," he admitted. "I would like to spend the rest of our days together, if you agree."

Korlue swallowed hard. The rest of his days was a grim thought, but he smiled. "We can open a little bookstore," he grinned.

"If that is what you wish."

Korlue nodded, fighting back tears. "I'll pack right away and be ready to go by the time you get back from Wales."

Raesh held him tight and kissed him fervently. The crowd seemed to notice the auspicious moment and cheered. A member of the waitstaff came over with two glasses of champagne as if to celebrate the happy couple. They clinked their glasses in a silent toast, then downed the contents and placed the empty glasses back on the tray.

When Korlue stumbled slightly, Raesh caught him. "Are you well?"

Korlue smiled crookedly. "I'm fine. I think I just had a little too much to drink. Perhaps a little air would help."

Raesh nodded and helped him back up. Then the room spun, and he nearly tripped. "I may have had too much as well," he laughed.

Members of the waitstaff were at their side when Raesh caught the familiar scent of blood on them. Before he could protest, he felt a sharp prick in his side, followed by the feeling of something toxic in his bloodstream. He looked over at Korlue as they were escorted outside, but he was barely conscious. There was a whisper of taking them to the Ausher mansion in Wales before he, too, slipped into unconsciousness.

# CHAPTER 19

B ronagh furrowed her brow in confusion. "But why leave the dragon behind?" she asked. "If those silly monks are going to drug him, we could just as easily take him."

"The dragon will probably wake before you get him to me. The Emori have never been good at keeping him sedated for long. And I want him panicked and desperate and willing to give himself over to me for the safety of his lover," said Dorjan. "I also need time to prepare for the final power transfer. I want no part of his soul left behind."

Bronagh and Eadan giggled, nodding their agreement before disappearing in a sliver of light.

They watched as they carried the unconscious dragon and his lover, a lightning elemental, out of a mansion. It was a massive structure, and there were many people going in and out. Some monks wore formal attire, while others wore servant's clothing. They took the dragon and the elemental out through the back, where there was no one watching. More of them were waiting outside. There were so many of them for just two people. It made Bronagh wonder how dangerous the pair were. Bronagh found it odd that the elemental was in a woman's dress when he was male. Though he did look lovely in it, even unconscious, but it caused the monks to struggle with carrying him.

Since they were to leave the dragon behind, they focused on the elemental. Bronagh could taste the energy coming from the elemental. His body buzzed with electricity, like the ionized particles in the air as a storm built up. It was the metallic tang of ozone. She grinned. His blood was not pure. He had the blood of the undead in him as well. A vampire.

"How delightful," she purred.

Eadan gave her a confused look, but Bronagh ignored it.

They waited until the group of monks were cleared of the building before they attacked. The monks had their backs turned to them as they loaded the dragon into a large metal wagon they had never seen before. Bronagh and Eadan transformed into their bestial skins, their bodies elongated, and their scales shimmering in the dappled moonlight, until they stood as towering serpents. They struck the two monks carrying the dragon's lover, their venom killing them almost instantly. They went down fast, and far too easily. Dorjan warned them not to hurt the elemental, so Eadan caught him before he hit the ground.

"Careful with him," Bronagh hissed.

"He's fine," Eadan snapped back.

The monks turned when they heard the commotion.

"Stop them!" one monk called out.

Eadan gently put the dragon's lover down, but stayed close as she and Bronagh prepared for a fight. Innocent bystanders, couples getting away from the party for some privacy, scurried away into the surrounding buildings. Bronagh and Eadan hissed as the monks surrounded them. The first monk, wielding a staff, swung his weapon, aiming at their heads. Bronagh dodged with whirlwind speed, her fangs bared as she lunged at him. The monk sidestepped, his movements fluid, and struck her side, causing her to recoil in pain.

Meanwhile, Eadan coiled around another monk, squeezing with immense strength. The monk, gasping for breath, muttered an incantation. A burst of light erupted from his hands, forcing Eadan to release him. He fell to the ground, coughing, but quickly regained his stance, ready to continue the fight.

An older monk with a calm demeanor raised his hands as he chanted a spell and summoned a protective barrier around Bronagh and Eadan. The serpents, now enraged, attacked the barrier with ferocity, their scales scraping against the near invisible shield. Two other monks joined in, chanting louder, their combined energy strengthening the barrier.

Bronagh and Eadan did not notice that the monks had gotten the elemental away from them, and were clumsily loading him and the dragon into the back of a strange-looking metal wagon.

Bronagh, realizing brute force was futile, transformed back into her human guise. She approached the barrier with a sly smile, her eyes glowing with dark magic. She whispered an ancient curse, and the barrier cracked. The monks, sensing the danger, focused their energy on maintaining the shield, but it was a losing battle. Panic and fear showed on their faces as the cracks spread.

Eadan turned back into her human form and joined Bronagh in her chant, and the barrier shattered. The girls grinned malevolently before returning to their full snake bodies. The monks, drained of their energy, were now magically defenseless. Even their martial arts skills were no match for Bronagh's and Eadan's speed and agility, and they were just too tired to put up much of a fight. Disappointment washed over Bronagh. The older monk, the last of them, fell to his knees as the serpents closed in on him.

With a sudden, forceful blow, they struck the older monk down. His once stoic figure collapsed to the ground—the strength of his will felled by brute force. The monks lay defeated, but not all dead, their bodies strewn across the street. Bronagh and Eadan, still in their serpent forms, made their way over to the metal wagon, wrenching open the doors with their tails. Eadan slithered in and wrapped herself around the elemental. They made their escape into the darkness and went back to Dorjan with their prize, cackling into the night.

# CHAPTER 20

The mountain stood tall against a vibrant sunset, its jagged silhouette slicing through the molten hues of the sky. Wisps of enchanted mist snaked through the rocky paths, swirling lazily as though echoing the whispers of ancient spells. A faint hum vibrated in the air—a sound almost imperceptible but undeniably magical, like the forge itself still sang with power. Wildflowers that seemed unnaturally vivid bordered the trail leading to the blacksmith's dwelling, their colors pulsating faintly with traces of magic. Shadows stretched long across the ground, weaving patterns that hinted at the unseen forces at play.

A week had gone by since Dorjan left the forge, and the mountain air was still heavy with the magic radiating from it. The path to the blacksmith's home was now a familiar one, but the presence of the illusion spell seemed stronger than before.

As Dorjan got closer to the forge, the weight of the spell pressed down harder on him, then the ghostly image of his granddaughter materialized once more, her eyes filled with a disturbing glee with a hint of rage.

"Hello again, grandpa," she grinned. "Why do you persist in this quest? That sword will only bring you pain."

"Why do you persist in trying to stop me from obtaining what's mine?" he argued. "I thought the gods were not allowed to interfere with a mortal's destiny?"

Her smile broadened. "But I'm not a god, and you are hardly a normal mortal. You're Fallen."

"And still mortal," he continued, trudging up the mountain path with some difficulty. "This spell is interfering with my destiny to reclaim my lost divinity. I will not be stopped."

"There's still time for you to turn back."

"Never!" he growled. His legs felt like lead weights as he climbed higher.

"This path of vengeance will be your undoing, grandpa," she purred. "I look forward to you joining me in oblivion."

The illusion laughed maniacally as it faded, the weight of the spell becoming lighter when he reached the entrance to the cave. Dorjan breathed in deeply once the weight was lifted. Entering the cave, he found Ulfberht at the forge, the newly crafted sword resting on the anvil, its blade shimmering with a faint magical glow.

Ulfberht turned to face Dorjan as he entered. "The sword is ready!" His brow furrowed at the sight of the exhausted look on Dorjan's face and his heavy breaths. "What has happened to you?" he asked worriedly.

"It is nothing. Just an awful spell trying to dissuade me from getting here."

"A spell? There is no spell on my mountain." He got up and retrieved a cup from his living quarters and filled it with water.

"Of course there isn't," Dorjan sighed, straightening up and accepting the water offered to him. He greedily drank down the water, then handed the empty cup back to Ulfberht. Wiping his mouth with the back of his hand, he pointed to the sword. "Is that it there?"

Ulfberht's eyes lit with excitement as he rushed back over to his work area to carefully gather up the sword and bring it to Dorjan. "Yes, I call it Valthorn, the Dragon's Legacy."

Dorjan had an expression of mild irritation. "There was no need to name it."

Ulfberht's laugh once again filled the cavern. "It is customary to name one's children at birth, is it not?"

Dorjan sighed with exasperation. "If you must." He took the sword and marveled at it.

The sword, Valthorn, as Ulfberht called it, was a breathtaking weapon, radiating an aura of ancient power and majesty. Its blade, forged from his dragon scale, was a deep, iridescent white with subtle hints of shimmering gold that caught the light of the forge's flames with every movement. The scale's natural patterns were still visible, creating an intricate, almost hypnotic design along the length of the blade.

Its blade was long, honed to a razor-sharp edge that could cut through the toughest of materials with ease. Reflecting the surroundings with an unearthly glow, the surface was smooth and polished to a mirror-like finish. A fine point, perfect for slashing and thrusting attacks, was achieved by tapering the blade's tip.

The hilt of the sword was crafted from a combination of enchanted metals and the finest leather. The cross guard was shaped like outstretched dragon wings, providing both protection and a striking visual element. Embedded within the center of the cross guard was a large, flawless diamond. Dorjan thought it was lovely, but wholly unnecessary. The weight of the sword was solid and reassuring in his hand, yet unnervingly light. The balance was impeccable, with the blade's center of mass perfectly aligned to flow with his movements, making it feel almost like an extension of his body.

And the grip was wrapped in dark leather, ensuring a firm and comfortable hold. It was adorned with intricate carvings of ancient runes, adding to the weapon's mystical appearance. The pommel was shaped like a dragon's head, with gleaming gemstone eyes. It truly was fine work, even if it did have a few unnecessary embellishments.

Dorjan could feel an added bit of strength emanating from the sword and flowing into him. It amazed him how much more powerful he felt holding the sword.

"I didn't sleep for days while forging this masterpiece," said Ulfberht, breaking Dorjan out of his reverie. "I have never had such pleasure crafting something so beautiful. Thank you for—"

Dorjan withdrew the blade from Ulfberht's stomach, and the large man crumpled to his knees as he tried to stop the bleeding with his hands.

Blood pooled from his lips, dripping down into his beard as he spoke. "Why?" he choked out.

Again, Dorjan sighed. "Because I wanted to." He grinned, snatching a cloth from off Ulfberht's tool belt to clean the blade. "And I needed to test out the blade."

"May the blade you wield be your undoing," he gasped, before choking on more blood.

As the life faded from Ulfberht's eyes, Dorjan stood over him, feeling... nothing. He was disappointed, thinking he would feel Ulfberht's soul dying, but he felt nothing at all. Grumbling, he took one last look at the forge as it grew silent; the flames flickering ominously. He left the cave with his new sword, and though he did not feel the death of Ulfberht's soul, he could feel his own power from when he was a god connecting him to the weapon. At least he did not kill the blacksmith in vain.

He descended the mountain with a lightness in his steps. The spell on the path was gone, Vala had either given up on trying to convince him not to continue on his journey or he broke the spell after killing Ulfberht. Either way, he was glad to be rid of pestering revenants of his past.

# CHAPTER 21

Raesh's eyes fluttered open, the dim light filtering in through the small, barred windows of the vehicle he found himself in. The cold metal of the chains bit into his wrists, reminding him of what happened. Wooden benches lined the sparse interior of the vehicle, where a few monks sat, their robes rustling softly as it moved.

Oblivious to Raesh's awakening, the monks murmured prayers under their breath; their voices humming low, blending with the engine's rumble. Raesh's heart pounded as he scanned the surrounding faces, searching desperately for his mate, but found no trace of him. His skin felt hot and tingly, his heart pounding louder in his ears, and his breaths coming out in short bursts.

With a deep breath, he tested the strength of the chains; they were made of an enchanted iron. He could smell the magic that burned with his movements. They would not give. He knew he had to act quickly. Summoning all his strength, he yanked hard; the chains clinking loudly as they strained against his muscles. The monks' heads snapped up, their eyes widening in alarm.

Before they could react, Raesh lunged forward, using the chains as weapons. He swung them with precision, the heavy metal links striking the monks with a force that sent them sprawling. The vehicle swerved as the driver struggled to maintain control, the sudden chaos throwing everything into disarray.

Raesh's movements were swift and calculated, each strike aimed to kill rather than incapacitate. They would pay for touching Korlue. The monks, though trained in combat, could not properly defend themselves against Raesh's raw power and rage in such close quarters. He took one by the head and pressed his thumbs into his eyes, squeezing until they popped, and blood splattered against the walls of the vehicle and Raesh's suit.

He quickly moved onto the last monk in the back with him and strangled him with the chains until his neck snapped. All three monks were dead within a matter of moments, and the vehicle was now eerily silent except for the labored breathing of the driver. With the guards neutralized, Raesh turned his attention to the chains. He searched the bodies for a key, finding a set on one of them, and unlocked the restraints, the heavy metal falling away with a satisfying clatter. Finally free, he moved to the back of the vehicle, pushing open the doors and leaping out into the night.

The cool air hit his face as he landed on the gravel road, the vehicle speeding away into the distance. Raesh took a moment to catch his breath, his mind already racing with thoughts of finding his mate. He did not understand why they were separated when they were being taken to the same place, but he would find Korlue no matter what. Even if he had to set every port on fire until he did.

He found himself in an unfamiliar part of town. The one time Aiden did not have his spies keeping an eye on him and he got abducted. He cursed under his breath as he scented the air; he was not even in the same state anymore. Where were they taking him if not to Roland Ausher? Where the hell did they take Korlue? He growled out in frustration. He would find his way back home to get help.

The sun had risen by the time he crossed state lines. The afternoon sun hung high when he made it back home. He let his rage fuel his journey, keeping him focused on his destination. His first stop was to Aiden's home. They all lived in modest houses on the enormous property he had bought for them. Many of the troop were milling about. Raesh found it odd that no one was getting ready to leave for Wales.

He shook his head. That was not important. He had to get to Aiden. Not bothering to knock, he marched right up to Aiden's home office.

"Andy! Good news, we're not going… what happened to you?"

"They took Korlue," he replied.

"Who took Korlue?" he asked worriedly.

"The Emori. They tried to take me as well, but I escaped." He went to the small bar Aiden had in his office and poured himself a drink. "I need your help to find him."

"Whoa! There's a lot to unpack here," said Aiden. "How did they even get you out of the hotel with no one noticing?"

"We were at an event, and they drugged us," he growled, making another drink and downing it.

"Take it easy there, friend. I need you sober right now," he insisted, taking the bottle of whiskey and sitting Raesh down.

"Please, Aiden," he pleaded. "Help me get him back."

"Of course I'll help you. We all will, but I need you to focus and tell me everything that happened to you in great detail. What all do you remember?"

Raesh relayed the events of the previous evening and what he remembered before he blacked out. "They said they were taking us to Roland Ausher, but when I woke up, I was a state over and Korlue was not with me," he explained.

Aiden nodded. "That is strange. They should have put you both on a ship immediately."

"What could they have done with him?"

"I'm not sure, honestly. We got a message canceling the performance in Wales."

"Do you think Korlue got away?"

"Not likely. They may not be able to handle you, but a waifish lightning elemental is pretty easy for them to contain," he said matter-of-factly. "Sorry, I don't mean to be insensitive, but I'm at a loss. My guess would be that they took him to a separate containment unit before taking him overseas. Keeping you two apart would be the smart thing, especially in case you escaped. They could use your mate as bait to lure you to them. That's what I would do."

Raesh narrowed his eyes at him.

"Hey, it was just an educated guess," Aiden said, his hands up in surrender.

"Then we go to Ausher," Raesh said, standing.

Aiden gave him a serious look. "That's exactly what they want, Andy. We need a plan."

"There is no time for that. We need to leave now," he demanded.

"They'll be ready for you to storm the castle in a blind rage. A cool head would be best to get Korlue back alive."

Raesh glared at Aiden, growling, but the wolf was unphased. "Fine, we do things your way," Raesh said after a few moments, sitting back down.

"Good, now you're being smart," Aiden replied.

Aiden went behind his desk and pulled a map out of the drawer. He spread it out on the desk and pointed to a large structure. "This is the Ausher mansion. The estate is massive and sits on a cliff. There are a great many entry points that we can take advantage of."

Raesh sat up, listening. Aiden went over what they could and could not do and how the Emori would form around the building. It was going to be difficult to find Korlue without anyone seeing them. They had to be smart about how they went about the rescue mission. There was always the possibility that Roland would join the fight should they be found out.

The last thing Raesh wanted was to face off with the god again, but Korlue was too important to him not to. He would just have to take the risk. He was going to get his mate back home safely one way or another.

# CHAPTER 22

D orjan stepped into the dimly lit basement, his presence commanding the attention of every shadow that danced along the stone walls. The air crackled with tension. At the center of the room, bound by rope, was the lightning elemental. His eyes glowed a fierce, electric blue, and arcs of lightning flickered across his skin, illuminating his defiant expression.

"Good evening, Korlue," Dorjan said, his voice smooth. "I am the god, Ozmir, but you may call me Dorjan."

Korlue's eyes narrowed at him, and without a word, he summoned a bolt of lightning, aiming it directly at Dorjan. The air sizzled as the bolt shot forward, but Dorjan remained unphased. With a swift, fluid motion, he raised his hand, and the bolt veered off course, spiraling around him harmlessly before dissipating into the ground.

"Impressive," Dorjan remarked, a hint of amusement in his tone. "But futile. Your power, while formidable, is no threat to me." He conjured a white flame in his hand, then made a fist, putting out the fire.

Korlue's expression shifted from anger to fear. "What do you want from me?" he demanded, his voice crackling like a distant storm. "Where's Andrew?"

Dorjan stepped closer, his eyes locking onto his. "Your dragon is not here," he grinned. "And he will not be coming. As far as he knows, the Emori took you, so he'll chase after them for a while. No one is coming for you."

The room fell silent, the only sound the faint hum of residual electricity. Korlue's defiance wavered, the storm in his eyes calming ever so slightly.

"Why?" Korlue asked, barely above a whisper as tears welled in his eyes.

Dorjan lightly took hold of Korlue's face. "Don't worry, I'll return you to your dragon in due time," he smiled wickedly.

Dorjan felt a sudden rise of lust within himself when he saw the hopelessness and fear in Korlue's eyes. He got in close and breathed in deeply. The scent of Korlue's fear was intoxicating.

"I can see why the dragon likes you so much," he murmured close to his ear, making him shudder. He burned the ropes off and took a step back. Then, with a malevolent look in his eyes and in a low growl, he said, "Run, little rabbit."

Korlue hesitated until Dorjan snapped his jaws at him. Then he bolted to the door, only to find it locked. Dorjan laughed maniacally as he slowly made his way to Korlue, who was frantically pulling at the door and screaming for help. Dorjan had noticed that he carried over some of Ahadiel's and Alexander's primal aggression and the need to hunt when he changed over to Rhianwen's body. He could not decide if it was a good or a bad thing, but coupled with the girl's lust and incessant need to feed, he found himself losing control and giving in to his baser urges.

Korlue sunk to the floor shaking, backing into the door as much as he could as he stared wide-eyed up at Dorjan. Dorjan could see the animalistic luster in his own eyes reflected in Korlue's, the pupils turning into slits. He towered over Korlue, a greater darkness welling with him.

"Please," Korlue begged. "I don't want to die."

Dorjan leaned over him. "Oh, I'm not going to kill you, little rabbit." He lightly cupped his face before roughly grabbing it. "But I am going to devour you," he said with a growl.

He dragged Korlue to his feet, and he struggled and clawed Dorjan's arm in an attempt to gain his freedom. The more Korlue fought, the more excited Dorjan became. Dorjan burned off Korlue's already tattered dress and undergarments, then tossed him away from the door. As he struggled to his feet, Dorjan stalked toward him with a frenzied look contorting his face. A barbed tail tore out of the base of his spine in a light spray of blood.

The tail whipped about behind him, and Korlue backed away into the far wall. Dorjan chuckled at the futile attempts to stay away from him. He raised his hand, and with a simple gesture, the shadow on the wall opened its blood-red eyes and took hold of Korlue by the wrists from behind. Korlue screamed, trying and failing to break the shadow creature's hold on him.

He froze the moment Dorjan got close. The shadow creature sprouted a second pair of hands that grabbed him by the ankles when Dorjan made another gesture with his hand. The hands lifted his legs, slowly spreading him wide and exposing him further. Dorjan took his other hand, and with a single finger, rimmed the entrance of Korlue's anus before penetrating him.

"So tight," he smiled. "Open up for me."

"No!" Korlue sobbed. "Please, don't do this!"

"Beg and scream all you like. It excites me." He undid his trousers and pulled his erection free. Lightly, he stroked himself, coating his cock in the precum leaking out of the head. Then he rubbed Korlue's thighs as the elemental continued to cry and beg for him to stop, but he could not stop, even if he wanted to. "Mm, so soft! I wonder, would you be more willing if I looked like him?" He took a step back and shifted his form. Muscles expanded as his skin changed to a pale tone, flecked in random patches with black scales that had an iridescent green sheen. His hair lengthened, turning from blond to black. As his facial features changed, his eyes took on an almond shape. He had transformed himself into Raesh. "How's this?"

Korlue took one look at Dorjan's changed form, then opened his mouth and screamed.

"Yes, just like that." He took hold of Korlue's limp member and stroked it until it hardened in his hand. "See, doesn't that feel good now? To have your lover caressing you so?" he asked in Raesh's voice.

Korlue sobbed ugly tears as Dorjan touched him with Raesh's hand. With his free hand, Dorjan positioned the head of his aching erection at Korlue's entrance, continuing to stroke Korlue until he came. When he stopped screaming, he was panting hard from his release. Now, with him relaxed, Dorjan forced his cock into Korlue, making him gag on a scream that got stuck in his throat. Dorjan withdrew himself partially and saw blood. Korlue was not as relaxed as he thought. At least now he had lubrication.

Dorjan pumped in and out of Korlue slowly at first, enjoying the sounds of his grunts and soft cries. His pace increased the closer he drew to his own climax, and he could feel Korlue's life essence flow into him. His energy tasted like despair and acquiescence. It was so delicious that he nearly took it all, but he somehow stopped himself and pulled out of him right before he came. Dorjan emptied his load all over the front of Korlue; he wanted to make sure Raesh and his overly keen sense could smell him all over his beloved. He wanted him to know what happened here. To know what his defiance would cost him.

Dorjan knew what he did was wrong and unforgivable, but he did not care. When Raesh next saw his lover, he would do anything to save him, even giving up his own body in exchange. And that was exactly what Dorjan wanted. He had to make sure that no part of Raesh's soul wanted to linger behind. His body would be his completely.

With that in mind, Dorjan put his cock away and had his shadow drop a now unconscious Korlue onto the cold, stone floor. He knew Korlue was half vampire, an elemental dhampir, and that he would not die so easily, but he would send a servant in to dress him and ensure that he survived. Korlue would need the blood to recover. Dorjan left the room, humming gleefully. His time in the mortal world would soon be over.

# Chapter 23

R oland paced the length of his office while Kezia watched him silently from the sofa. The Emori were due to arrive in a week with Raesh and his lover, but Thane had wanted to meet with him sooner to discuss something important. Roland had his concerns. He had never wanted a drink so badly.

"Calm down, my love," Kezia pleaded when he started muttering in agitation. "Brother Thane will be here soon."

He stopped and looked at his wife. She had a worried expression on her face. He walked over to her and knelt down, closing his eyes and relishing in the warmth of her hands when she cupped his face.

"I'm sorry, my love. I don't mean to worry you," he murmured. He took hold of one of her hands and kissed the palm. "I'm just a little nervous about all of this."

"As am I. I don't like any of this," she said, leaning her head against his. "What can I do to take your mind off of things until they arrive?"

He looked deep into her eyes and grinned. "I can think of one thing."

She frowned disapprovingly. "Roland, be serious," she fussed.

"You asked," he chuckled lightly. "But no, there isn't anything you can do to distract me right now." He gave her a soft kiss on the lips. "I appreciate the offer, though."

Again, she frowned. "Are you certain?"

"Yes, love," he smiled wryly.

They both turned when they heard a knock at the door.

"Are you two decent?" came Luxor's voice from a crack in the door.

"Yes," Roland sighed, giving Kezia another light peck on the lips before standing back up. "Enter."

Luxor came into the room, followed by Brother Thane. Thane had a somber expression on his weathered face.

"What happened?" Roland asked. "Are they here, or at least on the way?"

Thane shook his head. "We had them," he started solemnly, "but we lost them."

"How? How is it so hard to contain one dragon?" Roland snarled.

Kezia touched his arm, and he looked down at her pleading face, then took a calming breath and gave her hand a gentle squeeze.

"What happened? How did you lose them?" he asked calmly.

"It was Ozmir," said Luxor.

"Yes, he sent his familiars to take the elemental, but they left the dragon behind," Thane continued.

"Then what happened to Raesh?" Kezia asked.

"The sedative we gave him did not have a lasting effect, and he woke up sooner than we anticipated. He killed the guards that were escorting him to our safe house and broke out of his chains to escape," he explained. "Only the young driver was spared to relay the events of that night. We tried looking for them both, but had no luck in finding them."

It was all Roland could do to remain calm. He swore under his breath, glaring at Thane. "Now what? My brother is in possession of the one thing we needed to keep the dragon in line, and we don't even have the bloody dragon!"

"Roland!" Kezia fussed again. She turned and looked at Thane. "Does Raesh know my father has his lover?"

Thane took a moment to think. "I don't believe so. Elias stated they were both unconscious when the elemental was taken."

"Good," she nodded. "Then there's still a chance to lure him out here and capture him."

"So long as Ozmir thinks we have Raesh, that might work," agreed Luxor.

"So, it's back to our original plan, then? Have the circus come out?" asked Roland.

"That may not be necessary," spoke Thane. "I'm sure the dragon knows his lover was taken by us to bring here when we initially invited the circus. He'll likely come on his own."

Roland sighed, running his hand through his hair with his free hand. He looked down at Kezia again. "We need to prepare for a fight. There is also the chance that Ozmir will make it known that he has the elemental, then the dragon would go to him first." He paused for a moment, sadness in his eyes. "My brother will come for my wife and son to claim their lives. My family must be protected at all costs."

Thane nodded. "I understand. I will mobilize my people to converge here. We'll be ready for whoever shows up first." He bowed his head and excused himself.

Luxor lingered briefly before following Thane out of the office.

Kezia peered up at Roland with large silver eyes. "What are you going to do if my father shows up instead of Raesh?"

Roland took a seat beside his wife, still holding her hand. He looked at it; it was so small in his. "I will make sure you and Rhydian are safe," he said, kissing the back of her hand. "I'm going to kill my brother."

"Is that what you want to do?"

"No," he said flatly. "But I promised my mother, and I can't—I won't let Ozmir take you or Rhydian from me."

She leaned up against him, a sad smile on her face. "He's your family, too. Your twin. Are you sure there is no other way?"

He shook his head. "Ozmir is hellbent on killing us all for how he was treated as a god. Vala has a way of making things worse, and making him mortal did exactly that."

"If gods aren't allowed to interfere with mortal lives, why is she having you do her dirty work? You're still a god."

"I am, but I've been interfering with mortal lives for a long time. What's one more?" He did not want to tell her he would likely be punished for all that he had done in the time he had lived in the mortal realm. It was not the right time, and it never would be.

"I'm sorry you have to go through this. I wish there was more that I could do to help."

He gently cupped her face and kissed her passionately. "You're helping me more than you know, but making sure you and our son are safe would help me the most."

She nodded. "All right, we'll stay hidden until all of this is done."

"Thank you," he said, then kissed her on the forehead.

They sat there in silence for several long moments, just being with each other. He did not want to worry her with the possibility that he might die in this fight. His brother was better trained in combat than he was with the help of his familiars from when he was a god. Roland was more of a brawler and had no real head for battle tactics, especially recently. He would spend as much time as he could with his family before his brother came calling.

# CHAPTER 24

The Ausher mansion stood in front of them, an imposing edifice of stone and glass bathed in the silver light of the moon. Their aim was to get inside, find where they were keeping Korlue, and get out without being seen. However, nearly the entire troop came out with them. Those that could fight wanted to help Raesh and to be there should anything go wrong, but Raesh and Aiden would enter the mansion alone.

Raesh had remembered the tunnel on the side of the cliff that he had previously escaped from. It was possible that Korlue was being held in the same dungeon he once was. And now that he could freely use his wings, they could have gotten in that way, but Aiden did not think it was wise for them to fly in. Someone could spot them, even at night. So, they decided that the side servant's entrance was best. The rest of the troop had to remain hidden until needed.

Before they could get to the entrance, a small black cat crossed their path and sat in front of them. It had a perfect white teardrop on its forehead, and it growled and hissed at them, its golden yellow eyes glowing in the night.

"What are the chances of that just being a normal cat?" Aiden asked.

"None," Roland replied, stepping out of the shadows.

Aiden swore under his breath in German.

"Go," Roland started, looking down at the cat. "Protect my family."

The cat meowed, then vanished in a puff of smoke.

"Andy, we should run now," spoke Aiden, backing away.

"Where is Korlue," Raesh demanded.

"Not here," Roland answered. "The Emori lost you both. My brother has him."

Raesh's eyes went wide. "Please! You must help me get him back." Someone he did not know had his mate. Another god at that.

"Why would I do a thing like that?" Roland growled.

"Please, I will do anything."

Suddenly, the sounds of battle had started.

Aiden stood between Raesh and Roland. "Get out of here, Andrew," he said, his knives at his side. "The mad king known as Dorjan has your mate. Go. I'll hold Roland here for as long as I can."

Roland shared Raesh's confusion. Did he really think he could hold off a god? Before he could stop him, Aiden had launched his attack. He fought with the ferocity of a cornered wolf, his eyes locked on the enemy. Each of his movements was a testament to his training and resolve. He sidestepped a brutal swing from Roland, driving his blade into Roland's side with a grunt for his effort.

"Go!" he repeated, dodging another swing from Roland.

Raesh only hesitated briefly before he took off back to the front of the mansion. The moment he rounded the corner, he heard Aiden scream and what sounded like a fluid filled sack burst. Raesh gritted his teeth, tears falling down his face as he ran.

Blood and sweat mingled with the acrid scent of smoke assaulted his senses as soon as he reached the front of the mansion. He darted through the melee, seeing as he ran past, the order of monks, clad in simple yet sturdy robes, formed a disciplined line. Their eyes gleamed, and their movements were precise, almost choreographed. Each monk held a wooden staff, the ends reinforced with metal bands that shimmered ominously in the moonlight.

His troop of reformed mercenaries and killers were a motley crew against the orderly monks of the Emori. Some wielded swords and daggers, while others brandished whips, chains, and fire-breathing torches.

The monks moved as one, their staffs twirling and striking with blinding speed. Raesh watched as his friends and family, undeterred, charged forward with a roar. As the clash of bodies and weapons pressed on, the monks' disciplined training shone through as they deflected blows, their movements a blend of martial arts and sheer strength. One monk spun his staff in a wide arc, disarming Crow with a single, well-placed strike. Though Crow had been disarmed, he was not out of the fight. He lunged at the monk, transforming midair into a large tiger. He mauled the unsuspecting monk to death before moving on to the next.

Despite being outnumbered, the circus fought with a feral cunning. One female trooper, Julia, a lithe woman with a chain whip, lashed out with precision, wrapping her weapon around a monk's staff and yanking it from his grip. She followed up with a swift kick, sending him flying.

Nearby, the burly strongman, Bellamy, swung a massive claymore, cleaving through the air with lethal intent. A monk met him head-on, using his staff to parry and redirect the powerful blows. The fire-breathers were unpredictable. They spewed flames that licked at the monks' robes, forcing them to adapt their tactics. The monks moved with increased urgency, their staffs now working to extinguish the fiery assaults as well as repel physical attacks.

Raesh fended off a few monks that tried to stop his retreat from the battlefield, but Sacha, out of nowhere, removed the ground from beneath them. He watched as she made the earth swallow the monks, burying them alive.

"Andrew! Where's Aiden?" she asked, running with him.

"Dead. Killed by Ausher," he replied, his voice agonized. "I'm sorry, but I have to find Korlue."

"Go," she growled. "I'll cover you."

Sacha could not hide the fury in her eyes. She screamed, then turned back to fight the monks. Raesh could tell she was going to go after Roland if she could find him. She clashed with another earth elemental as he got further away from her. He kept going. Watching his partner die was not something he wanted to witness. He needed to get away before that happened.

There were many casualties on both sides, but Raesh could not think about that. He had to find Dorjan now and get Korlue back. With Aiden dead, the circus was finished. Raesh spotted Roland stalking angrily towards him, covered in Aiden's blood and other things, his hand directed at any who got in his way. With a gesture of his hand, a body exploded, blood and bones spraying in all directions. Raesh, overwhelmed with fear, ran and did not look back. His family was lost to him. He would not lose his only love as well.

# CHAPTER 25

R aesh kept running until he reached the far end of the Ausher property. He could still hear the fighting in the distance and feel the earth move as Sacha and the other earth elemental battled. He wanted to go back and fight. Sacha was stronger than she used to be as an elemental, but she was still only one person and there was only so much she could do before she ran out of energy. He should have gone back to help her, but Dorjan had Korlue, and he was in danger. Finding out that Dorjan was a fallen god unsettled Raesh, but it explained why he was so powerful and wanted him. Being a Lyr'kin for a Fallen was an awful fate. Now, his mate was tangled up in his mess.

"Oh good, you're still alive and free," came a familiar voice from behind him.

Raesh quickly turned around, then took a few steps back. When he looked to Dorjan's right, he halted his retreat. There stood two snake women, and one had her tail tightly coiled around Korlue. His bright blue eyes, once full of joy and laughter, were now dull and lifeless.

"Korlue?" Raesh whispered.

Korlue slowly raised his head, but it was like he was looking through Raesh rather than at him.

"What did you do to him?" he demanded, his voice trembling slightly.

"A better question would be what didn't I do to him," Dorjan replied, grinning. "He is quite delicious."

Raesh scented the air around Korlue, then growled, his hands in tight fists at his sides. "How dare you touch him!"

"You know, this all could have been avoided had you accepted your fate sooner instead of running off to join the circus," Dorjan said, an exasperated expression on his face.

"Let him go," Raesh said in a low growl, his fists suddenly engulfed in bright green flames.

"Ah, ah, ah," Dorjan warned.

The snake women giggled and Korlue cried out as the one that held him wrapped herself tighter around him.

"Stop it," Raesh screamed, as his heart pounded and a loud ringing filled his ears.

Dorjan sighed. "Your lover will get to live, but only if you turn yourself over to me."

Raesh hesitated. He did not know what to do next. Attacking Dorjan was out of the question, and he could not risk Korlue getting hurt if he attacked the snake women. There was no taking Korlue and running. He did not have a safe enough opening. There was only one option. He let a roar in anguish as his flames grew, enveloping him. His eyes met Dorjan's, the rage and uncertainty of Korlue's fate building within him. And with his head held low, his flames died out.

"Wise decision," Dorjan smiled.

The other snake woman slithered over to Raesh. Smiling, she clamped a set of iron manacles on his wrists. The manacles were enchanted and stronger than those the Emori used. The sudden feeling of being drained of most of his energy forced him to his knees. His whole body felt fuzzy on the inside, as if someone was rubbing fur on the inside of his skull, and it was all he could do to not throw up and stay conscious. He knew it was a temporary feeling, but it was unpleasant.

"Pick him up and let's be gone from here," Dorjan ordered. "My brother is close. We mustn't linger."

The snake woman grabbed the chains between his cuffs and forced him back to his feet. She dragged him along after Dorjan and the other snake woman that held Korlue. A wall of shadow appeared. It was wispy around the edges, and Dorjan stepped through it, followed by the other snake woman and Korlue as if it were perfectly normal.

"Come along, dragon," hissed the snake woman. She continued to yank at his chains and pulled him through the writhing portal.

His heart pounded in his ears, each beat echoing like a drum in the oppressive silence. The shadows seemed to stretch and twist around him. It was an ever-shifting labyrinth of darkness. Dorjan and his familiars moved with an eerie grace, barely making a sound as they led the way.

Every step that Raesh took felt like a tentative dance with the unknown. The shadows clung to him, whispering fears and doubts into his ears. He could feel the cold, damp air pressing against his skin, amplifying the chill that had settled deep within his bones.

His captor glanced back, his eyes glowing like twin flames of malice in the darkness. Dorjan must have seen the fear in his eyes because he was smiling. As they ventured deeper into the shadows, Raesh's mind raced with thoughts of escape, but the darkness seemed to conspire against him. Every flicker of movement was a potential threat, every rustle a reminder of his and Korlue's captivity. The shadows were alive, and they were watching.

The path ahead was uncertain, shrouded in a veil of darkness that seemed to stretch on forever. Raesh's breath came out in shallow gasps, his senses heightened by the deafening silence. He could hear the faintest of sounds— the distant drip of water, the soft rustle of unseen creatures. Each noise sent a jolt of terror through his body, something he had not felt in centuries.

Again, she pulled his chains, a silent warning that escape was not an option. Raesh's heart sank, the weight of his situation pressing down on him like a suffocating death shroud. He found himself trapped in a world of shadows, with no way out and no hope of rescue.

A dim light appeared in front of them, and they were exiting the tunnel of despair. And just like that, all the fear and anxiety was lifted, but now they were in a poorly lit stone room. Raesh looked to his left and saw multiple piles of ashes shaped like human bodies. The room smelled of blood and other bodily fluids—Korlue's and Dorjan's. Raesh felt his rage well up inside of him again. Dorjan had violated his mate, and there was nothing he could do about it.

"Well, at least you aren't pissing yourself with fear anymore," Dorjan grinned. "Take the elemental back to my bedchamber, and chain the dragon up."

"I will kill you!" Raesh roared.

"Yes, that's precisely what you'll be doing," said Dorjan, turning to leave. "Just not right now."

Before she could chain him to the wall, he snatched his restraints from the surprised serpent and charged after Dorjan, but before he could reach him, he found himself paralyzed where he stood.

Dorjan turned back around and made a tsking sound, then walked over to him. He roughly grabbed his face and got in close. "I have had your lover many times over since he's been in my care," he smiled. "You should hear all the pretty sounds he makes for me."

Raesh snarled and snapped his jaws, but that was all the movement he could manage. He was foaming at the mouth.

"Keep that rage, dragon. You're going to need it," he purred, then let him go, and turned to leave again. "Chain him up!" he commanded, ascending the stairs out of the room.

Raesh was hauled back to the far wall, where chains hung from the ceiling. He fought, but the manacles left him with only a fraction of his strength, and the serpent woman was much stronger than she looked. She unlinked the chains between his wrists and, with magic, they connected to the hanging chains and stretched his arms apart. Raesh howled and screamed as she slithered away, laughing. He was left alone, his chains rattling as heavy sobs racked his body. Death had finally come for him, but all he could think about was Korlue, and how he needed to save him and could not. He was going to die, and he would never see Korlue again.

# CHAPTER 26

The battle ended with a lone earth elemental on the opposing side. She was breathing hard, and was bleeding badly from one broken arm, but still she fought. The surviving monks surrounded her, closing in with their weapons. With one last desperate effort, she summoned earth pillars shaped like spikes, impaling several of her adversaries.

The remaining monks came down hard on her, each staff taking its turn striking her. She cried out as each staff made contact, her bones shattering with loud cracks and crunches. She lay silent on the ground, the earth beneath and around her soaked in fresh blood, her beaten body in a crumpled heap. Then the earth rumbled once more, and vines and roots sprung up, unfurling to wrap her body. Slowly, they sunk back into the ground, taking her body with them. They had reclaimed its own.

The fight was over, but they had lost. The dragon had gotten away, and Roland could feel his brother's delight at being the one to capture him. Ozmir was close by, but Roland could not locate him in time.

Roland took one look at his property. He would need to hire more earth elementals to repair the land after removing all the bodies. For now, he would prepare himself for the final battle to come. The neighbors were likely furious about the noise that night, and the fight between him and his brother promised to be equally chaotic. He did not look forward to the complaints.

When he went back into the mansion, Kezia immediately embraced him.

"Kezia? What are you doing down here?" he asked, holding her tight. "Where's Luxor?"

"Don't worry, I'm right here, and Lynnox is upstairs with Rhydian," Luxor replied tiredly. "Your wife is very disobedient."

Even in her weakened condition, Kezia still managed to be a handful.

"Come, my love. Let's get you cleaned up," she said, pulling Roland along.

Roland smiled when she stuck her tongue out at Luxor as they walked past him. Ever the brat, his wife.

Roland sat in their oversized quartz crystal tub, soaking and recharging as he tried not to let the weight of what he had to do crush his soul. His brother would soon have his immortal body, though it would not be complete until he had the power within Kezia and Rhydian. Fallen could not achieve godhood so long as they had a living mortal bloodline. Many Fallen atoned for their crimes by remaining mortal and enjoying their new lives. Ozmir was always the difficult one.

"I don't believe I wish to spend the rest of my life gazing upon such a sour face," Kezia spoke, breaking him out of his thoughts. Her expression softened when his did not change. "It's not your fault that Raesh escaped. He's always been slippery."

"And yet my brother managed to catch him," he frowned. "And soon, I will have to kill him."

Now she was frowning. "I don't want you to fight him."

He raised a curious brow.

"It's not that I think you'll lose, because I know you won't. It's just that you shouldn't have to kill your brother."

"Even though he had a blood curse placed on you and stole our only daughter so he could steal her body?" he reminded her.

She pouted. "Well, when you put it like that… He could burn for all I care, but it still feels wrong, though. At least for you."

He pulled her into his lap and kissed her. "We've discussed this already. I'm fine with it, love. Really."

"How? I know he's done awful things, but he's still your family."

"Technically, he's not anymore now that he's Fallen. And as far as I'm concerned, you and Rhydian are the only family I need."

She blushed at that.

"Besides, I promised to kill him so that you would wake up," he continued. "And I will not let him hurt either of you."

"I'm sorry you had to agree to that," she said with a solemn expression.

He lifted her chin so that she was looking at him again. "I told you, I'd do anything for you."

"Yes, yes. And you would drown the world if anything ever happened to me. I know that, but I'm always going to worry about you."

"Anything I can do to take your mind off things?"

She grinned. "I can think of one thing."

"Should we get out of the bath?"

"No, you're going to need the energy," she purred.

Before he could respond, her lips were on his. He held her in his embrace as she adjusted herself in his lap to straddle him. She raised her hips and sunk her cunt down on his erection, sheathing him inside of her tight warmth. He grunted at the feel of her around him, his hands sliding to her rear. They sat there, not moving, to get adjusted to one another. She usually needed a moment or two to get comfortable.

Once she was ready, she rolled her hips in a tight circle. Her mouth hovered above his as she rocked back and forth, her pace maddeningly slow. He lowered his head and nibbled lightly on her neck and collarbone.

She arched her back when he cupped her breasts and bit down on her neck. His bite was not hard enough to break skin, but enough to leave an impression.

As she ground her hips into him, his mouth moved to one of her breasts while one of his hands reached down between them. He pinched at the bundle of nerves between her thighs, making her gasp, then moan. She bucked as he licked and sucked her taut nipple and continued to twist and pull at her clit. She came undone with a weak shudder that made him growl with displeasure. He did not even feel her pull on his life force, and she was usually so vocal.

Either her mind was still focused on her worry for him or he was not doing his job well enough. He was intent on making her scream his name until the sun came up.

She looked down and met his dark gaze. "Roland, what are you—"

His mouth crushed hers in a heated kiss that left her dazed and gasping for air when he released her.

"You said I would need the energy," he reminded her, licking the side of her throat. "I won't stop until we're both spent."

She smiled devilishly at him. "We'll see about that."

His cock twitched when she squeezed him. "We'll see indeed."

They remained in the bath for another hour before moving to the bedroom. The sun was cresting as the night faded, but neither of them was tired of the other. True to the promise he made himself, Roland had her crying out his name until she finally passed out from pleasure induced exhaustion. He smiled down at her, completely depleted himself. She always took so much from him. Greedy little thing that she was. He laid down beside her, pulling her against him, and fell into a dreamless sleep.

# CHAPTER 27

The dim light from a single, flickering light bulb cast long shadows across the cold, damp basement. Raesh, his wrists raw and bleeding from the heavy chains, did not know how long they had left him down there. Alone. As he awaited his eventual death, he would occasionally see movement in the shadows. He even thought he saw the blood-red eyes of an Umbra, but he was not sure. No one gave him food or water since he arrived, so he might have been hallucinating. Soon, his body would burn out. Whether it was from starvation or dehydration, he was not certain.

The air was thick with the scent of mildew and despair; the walls echoing with the distant sounds of the city above.

Each passing moment felt like an eternity in his underground prison.

At the sound of voices in the distance, he raised his head, and the door creaked open with an ominous groan. In stepped Korlue, his eyes filled with a mixture of sorrow and what looked like defeat. He hesitated for a moment, as if he were gathering the strength to face the reality of Raesh's situation. The sight of him, bound and broken, must have sent a pang of anguish through his heart. Raesh had felt the same looking at Korlue's poor condition. He had been beaten and violated repeatedly. Raesh could smell it.

"Korlue," Raesh whispered, his voice hoarse from being in captivity without water. "You should not be here."

Korlue rushed to his side, kneeling on the grimy floor. "I had to see you. Why are you still here? I know you can escape."

Raesh shook his head, a sad smile playing on his dry, chapped lips. "I cannot leave. Dorjan will kill you if I do, but you need to leave this place. He has me now. You can go back home."

Tears welled up in Korlue's eyes. "You are my home. I can't leave you behind. Not like this."

"But you have to. It is not safe for you here."

Korlue's hand cupped Raesh's face, and he leaned into the familiar warmth.

"I won't leave you," Korlue whispered, the tears he was holding back finally falling. "I'll never leave you."

"Please, do not cry for me," Raesh spoke, holding back tears of his own. "I promise to find you again, in the next life. For now, you have to go. Live your life. Be free."

Raesh's heart ached with the weight of their impending separation. Korlue leaned in, pressing his lips to Raesh's in a tender, lingering kiss. It was a kiss filled with a love Raesh had never known until now. A longing and unspoken promise of a future together. The world outside ceased to exist in that moment. There were only the two of them, bound by love and fate.

As they pulled away, the sound of footsteps echoed down the stairs, growing louder with each passing second. Korlue's time was up.

He stood, his eyes never leaving Raesh's. "I will live for both of us until the next life."

Raesh nodded, his eyes shining with unshed tears. "Until the next life."

The door burst open, and the two snake women, now in full human forms, stormed in.

"There you are!" one hissed.

"Time to go!" grinned the other. "Our Lord has need of your body again."

They seized Korlue, dragging him away with brutal force.

Korlue struggled, his gaze locked with Raesh's until the very last moment. "I love you," he cried out, his voice breaking with emotion.

"I love you, too," Raesh called after him, his chains rattling as he struggled against them.

With one last, longing glance, they took Korlue away; the door closing behind them with a final, resounding thud. Alone once more, Raesh howled, fearing for Korlue's safety. The basement felt even colder now, the silence more oppressive. Heavy sobs racked his body as he cried out for his mate. All he could do now was cling to the memory of their last kiss and the warmth of Korlue's touch.

And in that dimly lit, desolate basement, Raesh whispered a vow to the shadows, "Until we meet again, my love."

The shadows snickered, and the red eyes appeared again, then disappeared. After a few long moments, screams broke the silence. Raesh pulled at his chains as hard as he could. The screams were coming from upstairs. It was Korlue. But no matter how hard he pulled, the chains would not move. He screamed into the void. Unable to break free, he could not save his love. He had never felt so helpless as he did in that moment. Dorjan was going to kill Korlue, and there was nothing he could do about it.

At least, not yet.

# CHAPTER 28

The basement was lit with flickering candles that cast eerie shadows on the damp walls. Dorjan moved with a calculated precision as he meticulously arranged the ritualistic items on the stone altar he brought in. The air was heavy with the smell of incense and ancient herbs, mingling with the underlying stench of mildew and burned human flesh—a smell he had recently grown accustomed to.

Everything had to be just right for his final transfer into his permanent vessel. He had to etch the symbols into the altar. Raesh's body was not a blood relation and required a slightly different ritual for the transfer. He was grateful to have kept Vitani's grimoire for this precise moment.

As he placed the last symbol, glowing faintly with an otherworldly light, he glanced at Raesh, who remained chained and weakened. The dragon had burned out a few times since he had been in captivity after seeing his mate. Dorjan knew he would need to feed once he had his new body, considering how awful Raesh looked.

His eyes gleamed with a sinister determination, the promise of immortality and revenge driving his every action. This was the culmination of centuries' worth of careful planning and preparation, a moment he had long anticipated. He would soon be a god again.

"Why so sad, Raesh? Do you not understand the honor you are about to bestow upon me?" he asked, his voice cold and devoid of empathy. "Who knew allowing you time to gain a genuine attachment would make capturing you so much easier?"

Raesh growled defiantly as he stared angrily at Dorjan.

A low, menacing chuckle escaped Dorjan's lips. "Glare at me all you want. It will not change your situation. Your body will soon be mine."

Dorjan reached for the ceremonial dagger—a beautifully crafted athame with an intricately designed hilt and a blade that glimmered ominously in the candlelight. The dagger was not just a tool, but a conduit for the dark magic that would transfer Dorjan's soul and powers into Raesh's body. He held it aloft, admiring its deadly beauty for a moment before returning his focus to the ritual.

Dorjan turned as the door opened and Bronagh brought Korlue in, with Eadan close behind.

"Excellent! Our special guest has arrived," Dorjan said gleefully as he watched the rage drain from Raesh's face to be replaced with fear. "Unchain the dragon and bring him to me, and keep the elemental close."

Bronagh nodded, smiling as she passed Korlue off to Eadan. The moment he was released, Raesh grabbed Bronagh. She squeaked and giggled at her situation.

"Kill her, and your lover dies," Dorjan said calmly before Raesh could bite Bronagh.

Raesh released her, the rage and defiance back in his eyes. Bronagh rubbed her neck before pushing Raesh in Dorjan's direction. Dorjan handed Vitani's grimoire to him along with the athame, noting his confusion.

"You are going to read this incantation," Dorjan started, opening the book to a specific page. "And then you are going to kill me with this dagger. If you do anything wrong, Eadan will kill your lover. Do you understand?"

Raesh looked over at Korlue, worry and fear in his bright green eyes. "If I do this, will you allow him to live and return him safely to his home?"

"No! Andy, don't do this!" Korlue cried out.

"Be silent!" Eadan hissed, tightening her grip on him.

Dorjan nodded. "You have my word that he will live and I will have him returned to his home."

Raesh sighed in defeat, his head held low for a moment. "Very well, I will do as you say." He raised his head, a hint of defiance in his expression.

"Good." Dorjan climbed onto the altar and laid down.

Raesh looked over the text before beginning the chant in an ancient, guttural language. Dorjan felt the dark power resonate within him as the symbols around the altar pulsed with energy, casting a blinding light that filled the room. He watched with satisfaction as Raesh's defiance wavered, the strange sensation of his essence being pulled from his body.

Pain contorted Raesh's features, but he refused to scream as he kept reading. Dorjan admired Raesh's resolve, knowing that he would soon break. The room seemed to spin; the shadows closing in around them as the ritual reached its climax. Dorjan's eyes locked onto Raesh's as the dragon plunged the athame into Dorjan's chest. With a final cry, Raesh completed the incantation.

The energy in the room surged, the bright light enveloping them both. Dorjan felt the transfer beginning, his soul leaving Rhianwen's body. The pain was excruciating, but it was a small price to pay for eternal life. As he felt his consciousness merging with Raesh's body, Dorjan reveled in the power that surged through him. He could feel Raesh's resistance, but it was futile. The ritual was too far gone, and soon, only a remnant of Raesh's soul remained. It was not what he wanted, but it would eventually fade away.

With a sense of triumph, Dorjan embraced his new existence. As the glaring light faded, he looked down at his new hands, flexing them with a sense of awe and satisfaction. He glanced at the altar, where Rhianwen's body lay, and watched as her form disintegrated into ashes.

At that moment, Korlue broke free of Eadan and ran over to him.

"Andy?" He looked up at him with hope in his eyes. "Are you all right?"

"Oh, I'm more than fine," Dorjan replied, a slow smile on his face. "But your dragon isn't here anymore." He looked at Korlue and watched as his blue eyes turned sad and filled with tears.

Korlue backed away in fear when Dorjan reached over to cup his face.

"Don't worry, I no longer have need of your body." He grinned as Korlue broke down, then a wave of intense pain shot through his new body. It was like nothing he had ever felt before. The need to feed. For blood. It was so strong.

He looked at Korlue with a feral look in his eyes, his fangs bared as he fell to his knees. His skin felt so hot, and there was pain between his shoulder blades and at the base of his spine. Bronagh and Eadan ran to his side immediately, and before he could stop himself, Dorjan grabbed Bronagh and tore into her throat. She fought him, but it was pointless. His venom soon paralyzed her.

"Bronagh!" Eadan screamed.

Dorjan looked up to see Korlue scurrying away as Eadan tried and failed to pry him off of Bronagh. As he continued to drain her, he reached over and grabbed Eadan by the neck. She clawed at his arm in futility. He was getting stronger as he fed on Bronagh, but it was not enough. He wanted more.

Once Bronagh was empty, he dropped her body and dragged Eadan to his blood-stained mouth. He greedily ripped into her throat, just as he had done Bronagh's. The wounds on his arm healed instantly.

His eyes met Korlue's as he continued to feed. Korlue's bright blue eyes were wide with fear and full of tears as he sat scrunched up against a far wall. One of the girls must have locked the door behind them.

After draining Eadan, he dropped her body and wiped his mouth with the back of his hand. He stood, straightening himself out. He regretted not feeding Raesh now, he no longer had familiars to do his bidding. Their bodies suddenly had a fair glow, then they shimmered out of existence. At least he did not have to dispose of them now.

He returned his attention to a fear-frozen Korlue, walking over to him. He offered him his hand. "Don't worry, I'm not going to eat you."

Korlue sat there transfixed, not moving. Dorjan sighed in exasperation, then reached down and yanked Korlue to his feet. With a wave of his hand, a wall of shadows appeared. He gripped Korlue tight and walked through the portal. He would keep his word and return the elemental home.

# CHAPTER 29

Lynnox, perched silently in the corner of the dining room, observed the Ausher family with a mixture of curiosity and relief. For the first time since Kezia had woken up from her long coma, the family was together, sharing a meal and laughter. Warmth and the comforting sounds of clinking cutlery and soft conversation filled the room.

Luxor lay curled up on a nearby chair, his ears twitching attentively. He, too, seemed to enjoy the rare moment of peace. Ozmir had been quiet, and there had been no attacks on the mansion in days. But he had his dragon, so they all knew a fight would soon be at their door. Until then, they would all enjoy their time together as a family.

As Roland raised his glass to make a toast, the cozy atmosphere was shattered. In an instant, he, Kezia, and Rhydian collapsed, their bodies slumping lifelessly onto the table. Panic surged through Lynnox. She leaped from her perch, transforming seamlessly from her feline form into her human guise.

"What happened?" she whispered, fear gripping her heart.

Luxor, sensing the urgency, darted to her side, his golden eyes wide in alarm. He quickly took his human form as well. They rushed to Roland's side, and Luxor checked for a pulse. It was there, but faint. Lynnox's mind raced with the possibilities, but only one stood out: Ozmir.

Her voice was steady despite the fear churning within her as she straightened herself up. "Lock the house down!" she commanded the household staff, her voice firm. "No one gets in or out until we know what's happened."

"This could be Ozmir's doing," said Luxor.

Ariel burst into the room, having heard the order. "What happened?" he demanded, his eyes scanning the scene with concern.

"I don't know," Lynnox replied, her voice shaking slightly. "But we need to secure the mansion and get this lot to safety. Help me get them to bed."

Ariel nodded, his powerful form moving with surprising gentleness as he lifted Roland. Together, with the staff, they carried the unconscious family members to their rooms, laying them carefully on their beds.

Lynnox hovered, ever the watchful guardian, refusing to leave their sides. Luxor joined her, his presence a silent reassurance. The hours stretched on, the mansion eerily quiet. Lynnox paced the halls, her eyes constantly darting to the bedrooms where her family lay. She checked on each of them repeatedly; her worry growing with every passing minute.

Soon, the hours turned into days, and none of them had yet to awaken. Dorian came out of Rhydian's room, a somber expression on his face.

"Anythin'?" Lynnox asked, hope in her tone.

Dorian shook his head. She patted the boy's arm, then told him to go get some rest.

"I'll let ya know if anythin' changes."

The young wolf nodded, then went off down the hall. She knew he would be back shortly. He had not left Rhydian's side in three days, and she did not think he would get much rest on his own. Lynnox sighed and sat back in her chair to work on her knitting. She needed to do something to ease her worry, or at least distract her.

The sun rose on the fourth day, and still none of them had woken up. And Ozmir had not shown himself. It was not until after the sun had long set that Roland stirred, his eyes fluttering open. Lynnox's heart leapt with relief, and she rushed to his side, Luxor close behind.

"Zaven, can ya hear me?" she asked, her voice trembling.

He nodded weakly, his voice barely a whisper. "Nox... Where's—"

"Shh, it's all right. Kezia's right beside ya and Rhydian's safe in his room with Dorian," she assured him, seeing the panic in his eyes ease away.

"What happened, Zaven?" Luxor asked.

"I'm not entirely sure," Roland said, sitting up with Lynnox's help. He happily took the glass of water she offered him and quickly downed its contents. "I think Ozzy's out of Rhianwen's body now. I can't feel him anymore."

Lynnox frowned. They had already mourned the girl's passing, only to lose her all over again.

"We need to be ready for when he comes." Roland attempted to get out of bed and was promptly pushed back down by Lynnox.

"Oh, no, ya don't," she fussed. "The house is secure. Ozzy hasn't bothered with us yet."

Roland sighed and stayed put, knowing better than to fight with her. When Kezia stirred, Roland immediately turned his attention to her. She had a look in her stormy gray eyes, glistening with unshed tears.

"I felt her die," she sobbed into Roland's chest when he held her.

"I know, love. I did, too," he murmured, rubbing her back gently as she cried.

Dorian burst into the room to announce that Rhydian was awake, and was pleasantly surprised to see Roland and Kezia were also up. He ran back to Rhydian, likely to report the good news. Lynnox sighed as she watched her charge console his wife. Then she looked up at Luxor and saw the worry in his golden eyes. She wondered if he was thinking the same thing she was. That, should Ozmir manage to kill Kezia or Rhydian, Roland would be easy prey when he fell into a deep sleep again. She and Luxor were no match for a god. They would lose the whole family because of their blood bond and there would be nothing either of them could do about it.

# CHAPTER 30

It had been four days since Dorjan had taken over Raesh's body. He had needed the time to acclimate to his final vessel. The initial disorientation had given way to a strange, almost electric familiarity. Unfortunately, he had also had to deal with the unfamiliar need for blood to heal. He had forgotten that his Andr were vampiric in nature, and that starving one would lead to a great need for blood or the body would have burned out. His familiars paid the price for his forgetfulness.

In his poorly lit basement, he practiced with relentless determination. He summoned his fire, the flames dancing at his fingertips and spiraling into infernos that scorched the walls. His fire was not completely white. It had a pale green undertone still, another reminder of the remnant of Raesh's soul still being present. The shadows, at least, obeyed his every command, shifting and twisting into dark tendrils that could ensnare and suffocate.

His shapeshifting proved to be somewhat of a challenge, but his body soon obeyed as well. He marveled at the fluidity of his new form, transforming into various creatures and human disguises with ease. The only issue he had with his changes was that his eyes remained the same, blazing green. It would be difficult to get past his brother's security with such an obvious trait that was unique to him now.

By now, Zaven would have noticed that he was no longer in Rhianwen's body. Though they could no longer sense each other, Zaven would be ready for him. Dorjan was not at his full god power yet. He needed an edge in the coming battle with his brother. The sword he had made from his scale was truly a captivating work or art. Forged with the intent to kill a god, its blade shone with an ethereal light. He practiced tirelessly with the weapon, feeling its immense power resonate with his own. The sword responded to his movements with an almost sentient awareness, cutting through the air with deadly precision.

As the days passed, his confidence grew. He felt the strength of his powers solidifying within him, each ability honed to perfection. Yet, despite his newfound prowess, he could not entirely ignore the flicker of Raesh's presence within him. He could still feel the longing the stubborn ember felt towards his lost love. But Dorjan had no time for such sentimentality. His focus had to be on the imminent confrontation with his brother.

On the fourth day, he stood in front of a mirror, gazing at his reflection. The face that stared back was Raesh's, but the eyes were his own—cold, calculating, and filled with a ruthless determination. He tightened his grip on the sword, feeling its power thrumming in his hand.

"I'm ready," he whispered to himself, his voice a low growl. "It's time to end this."

With a final, confident stride, Dorjan left the room, his mind set on killing his twin. Though he was not at full strength, the powers he wielded were formidable, and he was prepared to use them without hesitation. The remainder of Raesh's soul could wait—his destiny lay ahead, and he intended to seize it with both hands.

# CHAPTER 31

*H*e stood in the middle of the grand celestial court, bound in chains, as the air crackled with divine energy. The other gods, their forms radiating with an ethereal glow, looked down upon him with stern, disapproving eyes. His brother Zaven, however, was notably absent, unaware of the events unfolding in the celestial realm.

"Ozmir," spoke the chief god, his voice resonating through the chamber like a thunderclap. "You stand accused of causing the death of a mortal and interfering with their destiny. How do you plead?"

Ozmir lifted his chin, defiance burning in his eyes. "I plead guilty," he said, his voice steady. "But I did it for the greater good. The mortal had ensnared my brother's heart and caused him to neglect his duties."

*Among the spectators, Vala watched with an icy gaze. She had never liked him or treated him as well as she did his twin. Everyone knew she favored his twin, and now her disapproval was obvious.*

*The chief god's gaze hardened. "You have overstepped your bounds and disrupted the natural order. Your actions have caused irreparable harm."*

*Ozmir's mind flashed back to the moment he orchestrated the death of Zaven's mortal wife, believing it would force his brother to return to his divine duties. He had not anticipated the depth of Zaven's grief or the impact it would have on the mortal world. So many had died in those four days.*

*The guilt weighed heavily on Ozmir, but he masked it with a façade of conviction. "The mortal realm is where our influence is needed most," he argued. "My actions were a means to an end."*

*Vala's expression remained cold, her disdain for him evident. She had always thought him unworthy of the divine lineage. His siblings were no different as they whispered among themselves.*

*The chief god raised a hand, silencing the court. "Your intentions do not absolve you of your crimes. For your transgressions, I banish you from the celestial realm and you shall become Fallen," the chief god declared.*

*"No!" Ozmir shouted. "That's not fair!"*

*"Perhaps some time living as a mortal will humble you," said the chief god.*

*"And what of my brother? Will he be Fallen as well?" he asked in his panic.*

*The chief god thought about his question briefly. "No," he said simply. "Your brother was a victim in this crime."*

*"But Zaven killed—"* The chief god put his hand up to silence him.

The verdict hung heavy in the air, and Ozmir felt the weight of his punishment settle upon him. The other gods chanted in unison, their voices weaving a powerful incantation. Light enveloped Ozmir, and he felt his divine essence being stripped away, leaving him vulnerable and mortal.

As the incantation reached its climax, Ozmir felt a searing pain unlike anything he had ever experienced. A force tore his powers from him, dividing them into four vessels and scattering them across the mortal realm. The celestial court faded from his vision, replaced by a swirling vortex of light and darkness.

Ozmir felt himself falling, plummeting through the realms with terrifying speed. The sensation was disorienting, a maelstrom of emotions and sensations overwhelming his senses. He struggled to hold on to his identity, to remember who he was, but the force of the fall was relentless.

When he finally landed, it was not with a crash, but with the gentle cry of a newborn baby. Ozmir opened his eyes to a new reality, his once powerful form now that of an infant. The memories of his trial and banishment remained, but his powers were gone, save for his fire, and he was now reborn as a mortal.

A woman, unaware of the fallen god she held, cradled the infant Ozmir in her arms and cooed softly. The world around him was strange and unfamiliar, a stark contrast to the celestial realm he had once called home. He felt the vulnerability of his new form acutely, the helplessness of infancy a bitter reminder of his fall from grace.

*As he grew, the remnants of his past life simmered beneath the surface, a burning determination to reclaim his lost powers and seek revenge against those who had cast him out. He knew that to restore his power, he would need to find the four vessels that contained his powers. They would be marked with the symbol he bore on his chest, a flame wrapped in a crown, on top of an infinity Ouroboros.*

Dorjan shook off the memory, refocusing on the present. The power he now wielded was a means of reclaiming his lost glory and settle old scores. The confrontation with his brother and family was inevitable. And this time, he would ensure that he emerged victorious.

The Ausher mansion stood against a backdrop of a stormy sky. The tension in the air could be felt as Dorjan, now fully acclimated to Raesh's body and the power it held, approached the already battle-worn front lawn. His footsteps echoed ominously on the broken cobblestone path, a herald of the chaos to come.

The wind howled, and dark clouds gathered overhead. Roland awaited by the mansion's front gates. The residents of the mansion had retreated to safety. Dorjan stepped into the open, his presence commanding and menacing. The light of the moon flickered in and out as clouds passed, casting dark shadows on his determined face. He could feel his power within him, ready to be unleashed.

Roland faced him, his expression unreadable. "Ozmir," he said, his voice holding a slight edge to it. "This ends tonight."

Dorjan's eyes shone with a malevolent glee. "You're right, brother. It most certainly will."

With a swift motion, Dorjan summoned flames that roared to life around him, their heat intense and blinding. Shadows twisted and coiled at his command, forming dark tendrils that reached out to ensnare Roland. The storm clouds above rumbled, a dark prelude to the battle.

Roland raised his arms, and water surged from the clouds and the surrounding plants, forming a protective barrier around him. The water swirled and danced, shimmering with an otherworldly glow. With a powerful gesture, he directed a torrent of water toward Dorjan, the force of the attack matching the intensity of the flames.

The two brothers clashed in the midst of the storm, their powers colliding in a frightening display of strength and skill. Fire met water in a fierce battle, steam rising as the elements warred against each other. Dorjan lunged at Roland, his sword in his grasp, its blade slicing through the air with lethal intent.

Roland parried the strike, the water swirling around him in a protective cocoon. He countered with a powerful wave that knocked Dorjan back, the force of the impact sending him flying across the yard. But Dorjan was relentless, summoning shadows to bind his brother and launching another fiery assault.

Roland roared as the flames hit him, searing the flesh of his arm and part of his chest, forcing him to his knees. Dorjan's shadows held him fast, and he hastened his approach, his sword in hand. Before he could deliver a killing blow, Roland wrenched himself free of the shadows and narrowly dodged the strike, the sword slicing the upper part of his arm. Dorjan grinned when Roland noticed the wound was not healing with his magic and was bleeding badly. The fear in his eyes as he put distance between them was delicious. The realization that the sword was a god killer was written all over his pale face.

"Where did you get that?" Roland asked, bewildered.

"I had it specially made just for you and our rotten family," Dorjan replied gleefully.

Roland's eyes went wide. "You can't be serious, Ozzy! This is madness!"

"You have no one to blame but yourselves for what's coming," he growled.

His brother was wounded and scared now. This was his chance to finally end things. Dorjan ran at Roland, putting his brother on the defensive. Roland used his water to deflect another swing from Dorjan's sword, backing away and trying to keep his distance from the dangerous blade. But Dorjan would not go easy on him. Long gone were the memories of the love he once had for his brother.

The battle raged on, each brother pushing the other to their limit. The already worn lawn bore the scars of their conflict. Their fight scorched and waterlogged the plants, and tore the ground apart.

Despite his immense power, Dorjan could feel the strain of the fight. The parts of Raesh's soul that remained stirred within him. Still, Dorjan fought, slashing and stabbing at his brother. Then the sword was suddenly heavier. He could not move it for a moment. And as his control wavered, he remembered Ulfberht's words. The sword had turned on him at the worst possible time. Roland seized the moment.

With a final, decisive move, Roland's eyes glinted with a fierce intensity as he extended his control over water to the blood flowing within Dorjan's veins. Dorjan felt an unimaginable pain as his very life blood responded to Roland's command, paralyzing him. His sword clattered to the ground, and Dorjan fell to his knees, gasping for breath.

"It's over, Ozzy," Roland said, his voice tinged with regret. He picked up the sword. "I'm sorry."

Dorjan, now vulnerable and defeated, struggled against the overwhelming force controlling his body. With eyes wide, he watched as his brother pulled the sword back, then thrust it forward into him. Roland released him from his hold on his blood, pulling the sword free of his body, and caught him before he hit the ground. He cradled Dorjan in his arms as he coughed up blood.

"I didn't want this for you, Ozzy," he said, a tear falling down his face. "Why couldn't you just be happy as a mortal like the other Fallen?"

Dorjan choked up more blood as he tried to speak, but could not. He wanted to tell his brother that he could never be happy as a mortal, not like he had. That his life as a god was the only thing that ever meant anything, at least when he had him by his side. All he wanted was to have his brother back with him.

Now he was just tired. He could hear Roland—no, Zaven, his brother's name was Zaven—calling for him in the distance. His voice was so faint now, and everything was so dark, but he felt warm all over. Then he felt nothing at all.

# CHAPTER 32

Roland quickly laid his brother's body down as white flames with a pale green tint engulfed him, leaving behind nothing but an ashen husk. He sat there in silence for a few moments. This was not what he wanted.

The sky was beginning to clear, the storm clouds parting to reveal the first hints of dawn. Roland turned away from the husk, his heart heavy with the weight of his actions. He had done what was asked of him, and his family was safe, but the victory felt hollow. The loss of his twin, despite all that had transpired, left a void within him.

"Well done, Zaven," came a familiar, lilting voice from behind him.

Roland frowned, picking up the fallen sword. He felt her take a step back before he turned to face her. "Vala," he said, his voice cold. He stepped around her, but she lightly placed her hand on his shoulder to stop him. "What?" he growled, not looking at her.

"You made a promise to me," she said. "I've come to collect on your debt. I hope you haven't forgotten."

"I remember," he sighed.

"Good, then come along."

He turned to face the woman that brought him into existence, his expression holding no love for her. "I need to say goodbye to my family."

"You should have done that sooner."

"I know, but it was never the right time. Please, I need to see them. To let them know I survived and that I must leave."

Vala's eyes flickered with a hint of emotion, something akin to irritation, perhaps even pity, but it was quickly masked. "You have one day," she declared, her tone leaving no room for negotiation. "Use it wisely."

He gave a curt nod.

"And I'll be taking that," she said, pointing to the sword he held.

He handed it over to her reluctantly, knowing no good would come of her having a weapon that could kill a god, but it would not be safe in the hands of mortals, either.

"What will become of my brother's soul?" he asked.

Her mouth was a line across her beautiful face as she thought about the answer. "His soul was destroyed. This sword made sure of that."

With the sword in hand, she turned and disappeared into the morning light, leaving Roland alone with his thoughts. He knew his time was limited, and there was much to do.

Lynnox and Kezia greeted him with worried faces as he entered the mansion, Rhydian and Luxor close behind.

Kezia immediately embraced him, and he could hear her faint sobs in his chest. He wrapped his arms around her, unsure of how he was going to break the news of his having to leave her. Gently, he pulled her away from him and cupped her face.

"I'm all right, my love," he murmured, brushing a tear from her cheek.

"Is it finally over?" she asked.

He smiled as he nodded. "Yes, it's over," he replied, then kissed her.

"Father, you're hurt," spoke Rhydian, approaching his parents.

Roland met his son's gaze. "It's just a few burns and a cut. I'll heal." He held his arm out to his son, then hugged him with his mother.

He knew he needed to tell them all about his impending departure, but he could not bring himself to break the news just yet. Instead, he would wait, savoring the precious moments he had left with his family.

The mansion's atmosphere radiated with warmth and love. Kezia sat in the living room with Rhydian. Their laughter echoed through the halls as they shared stories. Roland joined them, determined to make the most of the time they had left together. He had spent a few hours locked in his office signing paperwork that would transfer his funds and business over to Rhydian. Luxor eyed him with suspicion, but said nothing. Roland was grateful for it.

The afternoon and evening passed in a blur of laughter, games, and cherished moments. Roland watched as Kezia and Rhydian interacted. Their bond had grown strong in a short amount of time. He could feel the clock ticking down, but he pushed the thought to the back of his mind, focusing on the present.

After dinner, Rhydian excused himself, a mischievous glint in his eyes. "I have a surprise for the both of you," he grinned, disappearing down the hallway.

Roland and Kezia exchanged curious glances, wondering what their son had planned.

Moments later, Rhydian returned, carrying his father's cello. Roland had always known the boy admired his playing and had been practicing with it for several years. Rhydian carefully positioned the instrument, bow in hand, and looked at his parents with a mixture of excitement and nervousness.

He took a deep breath and played, the rich, soulful notes filling the room. The melody was one that Roland had often played for Kezia during her coma, a song of love and hope. As he played, the beauty of the music resonated through the house. Roland felt a lump in his throat as he listened, the familiar strains of the cello evoking memories he had mostly buried. Kezia's eyes filled with tears, her hand clutching Roland's as they shared in the moment.

The music swelled, each note a testament to Rhydian's dedication and love for his family. As the final notes faded into the evening air, he looked up, his eyes glistening with unshed tears.

"I hope you liked it," he said softly, his voice trembling.

Roland and Kezia stood and approached their son, their hearts overflowing with pride and love.

"That was beautiful, Rhydian," Roland spoke, his voice thick with emotion.

Kezia embraced her son, her tears flowing freely. "Thank you, Rhydian. We will cherish this memory forever."

Rhydian smiled, relieved and happy to have given his parents a moment of joy.

As night fell, Roland knew the time had come to say his goodbyes. He led his wife and son out to the gardens, the stars above twinkling like diamonds in the night sky. Finally, as they reached a quiet, secluded spot, he knew he could not wait any longer.

"Kezia, Rhydian, there's something I need to tell you," he began, his voice tinged with sorrow and regret.

They both looked at him, their faces filled with concern.

"What is it, Roland?" Kezia asked, her grip on his hand tightening.

Roland took a deep breath. "Remember the promise I made to my mother to wake you?"

Kezia nodded. He could feel her worry growing.

"Well, that wasn't all of it." Again, he took a deep breath. "I also had to promise to return to the celestial realm. I have to leave, and my time is running out."

Kezia's eyes went wide, and Rhydian's face fell.

"What? You're leaving us?" Rhydian's voice quivered in disbelief.

"I'm so sorry," Roland said, his heart breaking at the sight of their pain. "I would have told you sooner, but I didn't want to ruin our time together."

Tears welled up in Kezia's eyes as she stepped closer to him. "You should have told us. We could have prepared ourselves."

"I didn't want to take away from the joy of us being together," he explained, his voice trembling. "I wanted to cherish every moment with you both."

Rhydian, his emotions raging within him, stormed off.

"Rhydian, wait!" Roland called after him, but he was gone.

"How long?" Kezia asked, scowling at him.

"I leave in the morning," he replied, looking down at her.

Her expression was one of hurt and anger, and he only had himself to blame for it.

"Kezia, I—" His words were cut short when she slapped him across the face, then she too was gone.

Roland went back inside, each step feeling like a leaden reminder of the increasingly short time he had left.

"Zaven Lareceun!"

Roland groaned at the sound of Lynnox's shrill tone. He was in no mood to be yelled at. "Not now, Nox."

"Yes, now," she fussed. "What's this I hear about us havin' to go back to the celestial realm?"

"Not us," he sighed, running his hand through his hair. "Just me. You and Lux will stay here and care for my family."

"I knew there was something going on with you," said Luxor. "Why weren't we told of this? Or are we not your family, too?"

"You are, and I'm sorry."

"That's not good enough, Zaven," he hissed. "Your family deserves better than that."

Roland hung his head in shame. Luxor was right, they did deserve better. They had done so much and put up with more than they had to over the centuries. He could have at least told his familiars and trusted them with his burden. Perhaps it was for the best that he was leaving.

"You're right, you all deserve better than what I've given."

Lynnox's expression softened. "Oh, lay off him, Lux. He's been beat up enough."

Luxor scowled. "There you go, coddling the boy again."

"Of course I am! That's what mums do," she smiled. "They also forgive."

Luxor huffed, throwing his hands up, then left.

Lynnox patted Roland on the arm. "Go on, love. See to yer missus and son. They're in their rooms."

He gave her an apologetic smile. "Thank you, Nox."

"And don't worry 'bout 'em. Lux and I will take good care of 'em till ya get back."

"I know you will." He surprised her with a hug and a kiss on the cheek before he ran off back inside and up the stairs.

When he got to the main hall, he stopped at Rhydian's room first, but heard him talking to Dorian. So, he kept going until he reached his room. He felt it sadly familiar; him standing outside the door, hesitant to go in because she was once again angry with him.

With a heavy sigh, he pushed open the door. He was happy she no longer kept knives under her pillow. Such things had been put away long ago. He stood in the doorway for a moment to admire her. He half expected her to still be awake and fuming, but she was sound asleep. Exhaustion had won out, as she had likely cried herself to sleep. There were a few broken vases and dents in the walls from where they had hit, leaving water and flowers strewn across the floor among the shattered porcelain. Quietly, he padded his way over to her. He pulled back the blanket and crawled into bed behind her. Instinctively, she turned and curled into his arms. She groaned as her eyes fluttered open, pushing away from him when she realized he was holding her.

"I didn't mean to wake you," he sighed. "You should go back to sleep."

"I'm not tired anymore," she replied, stifling a yawn.

He smirked at her lie.

"What are you smiling for? You're abandoning us," she hissed.

He frowned. "I'm not abandoning either of you, Kezia."

"You're leaving."

"Yes, but not tonight," he retorted. "And I don't want to spend my last night here fighting with my love."

Her features softened at his words. "I'm sorry," she sighed. "Is there no way you can stay?" she asked after a moment.

"I'm afraid not." He gathered her back into his arms when tears fell from her stormy gray eyes. "I'm sorry. It has to be this way, my love."

"Please," she begged, choking on sobs. "Don't leave me."

He choked on his own tears. "I don't want to leave you, but it was the only way to bring you back."

She continued to cry, and he held her until she was done.

"What will we do with you gone?"

"Live," he murmured. He gave her a lingering, gentle kiss, pulling her closer to him.

She broke their kiss, peering up at him with tears in her eyes again. "Make love to me. One last time."

He answered her request with another kiss, this one more passionate and full of need. Desperate and hungry for her, he quickly got up and removed his clothes. She welcomed him back into her arms; her need matching his. He kissed and nipped at her lips and neck, coaxing breathy sighs and moans from her.

They spent the rest of the night making love, and he doted on and spoiled her tirelessly, making her cry out for more in ways he did not even know he was capable of. He loved on her until she could take no more of his sweet torture, silently promising to return to her one day.

The next morning came far too soon. The golden rays of the sun beamed down through the window to signal the start of a new day. But it was not a happy dawn. It heralded Roland's departure. Vala would be there soon to take him away from all that he loved.

He lightly brushed a stray curl from Kezia's face, then kissed her cheek. "Time to get up, love," he murmured against her skin.

She groaned her disapproval at being roused from sleep.

"Come on, pet," he chuckled.

"No," she whined.

He smiled. "Why not?"

"Because," she started, opening her eyes. "It will be tomorrow, and you'll be gone."

"I'm still here," he replied.

"For how long?"

He frowned at that. "I honestly don't know."

A gentle knock came at the door.

"Enter," Roland called.

Lynnox came in. Her eyes were red and puffy. She must have been crying all night. Still, she smiled.

"Breakfast is ready," she announced, her voice hoarse.

"Thank you, Nox. We'll be down shortly."

She bowed, then left.

Roland convinced Kezia to get out of bed, though neither of them felt hungry. They made their way downstairs to the main dining hall where Rhydian and Dorian were waiting along with Lynnox and Luxor. A large spread of food awaited them, yet no one seemed inclined to eat any of it. They all sat quietly, too sad to speak.

Dorian's stomach rumbled loudly, and he blushed hard. His already tanned skin turning bright red. The room erupted in laughter, and then everyone filled their plates and ate.

After an hour of clinking cutlery and light conversation, Vala appeared, her light warm and radiant.

Lynnox and Luxor bowed immediately in her presence. Everyone else stood and gathered around Roland.

"It's time, Zaven," she said, her voice echoing with an otherworldly resonance.

"Please, I need more time," he pleaded, holding Kezia and Rhydian close.

"Of course, and I can always put that one back to sleep," she said, a cruel smile playing on her pristine face. "Then you would have killed your brother for nothing."

"No," he breathed in shock.

"Then a promise made is a promise kept."

With a final, lingering kiss to Kezia's forehead, Roland stepped away. He looked at Rhydian and placed both hands on his shoulders, smiling at him. He had grown so much, now a man was standing before him. "Take care of your mum for me, all right?"

Rhydian fought back his tears as he stepped forward and hugged his father fiercely. "I'll miss you, father."

Roland patted the side of his face, feeling the stubble that had grown in. "I'll miss you, too."

When Roland moved to join his mother, he turned to his family one last time, his heart heavy. Rhydian held his sobbing mother as she broke down in his arms. With a longing glance at those he loved, Roland and Vala ascended, their forms fading into the celestial light.

# CHAPTER 33

And just like that, his father was gone. Really gone. Rhydian would now bear the weight of his father's absence as he worked to console his mother. He knew the pain of losing Roland would be unbearable for her, and he resolved to be her pillar of strength.

Kezia went limp in his arms, and he picked her up. She was still so frail, especially now.

"Come, mother, let's get you to bed," he whispered, carrying her up the stairs as she cried in his chest.

When he got to her room, he laid her down and tucked her in. He sat by her side until she cried herself to sleep. Lingering there for a few moments; he understood her pain. Having spent most of his formative years without the guidance of his father.

With a heavy sigh, he stood to leave, giving his mother a light kiss on the forehead. When he went back into the hallway, Dorian and Lynnox were waiting for him.

"How is she?" Lynnox asked, her face full of worry.

"As well as to be expected, all things considered," he replied.

"And how are you?" asked Dorian, taking his hand in his.

Rhydian shrugged. "I'll be fine," he said, his expression apathetic. "I'm used to him not being around, anyway."

"Oh, Rhydian," Lynnox frowned.

"Really, I'm all right. It's my mother I'm worried about."

Dorian raised Rhydian's hand to his lips and gave it a gentle kiss. "She has you. She'll be fine. I'm sure of it," he smiled.

Rhydian returned his smile, then leaned over to kiss him. Lynnox blushed at the pair before bowing her head and leaving. She had promised to check on Kezia later when she had the chance. Life at the Ausher mansion would have to go on without Roland.

The morning after Roland's departure, Luxor approached Rhydian with the news that would change his life. He informed him that his father had left the business and all his assets to him. Rhydian took on a significant role in Ausher Apothecary, working closely with Luxor to ensure everything ran smoothly. Dorian's contributions were equally vital during the transitional phase. With his deep knowledge of botany and pharmacology, Dorian played a crucial role in helping Rhydian understand the unique properties of the plants and ingredients that formed the foundation of their products. His patient explanations and hands-on demonstrations allowed Rhydian to grasp the intricate processes behind the craft, instilling in him a newfound appreciation for the art of apothecary work.

They poured their hearts into the business, creating new remedies and potions that helped their customers in different ways. They even designed apothecary cards—beautifully illustrated guides that detailed the uses and benefits of various concoctions and herbs. The cards became a fantastic addition to their service, providing valuable information and a personal touch to their clientele.

Despite his busy schedule, Rhydian was actually feeling the void left by his father deeply. Though he was reluctant to admit it, he missed the man. To cope with the sense of loss, he went to visit the mermaids. He wanted to recreate his father's tincture to help both him and his mother. She was refusing to get out of bed and she barely ate anything. Though it would not be the same as the one his father made, and it would not have his power to enhance it. At least his mother would not get addicted to it like she did with the last batch.

One crisp morning, Rhydian set out for the secluded grotto where the mermaids resided. When he arrived, they greeted him as they would Roland.

"Rhydian!" they spoke in unison.

"Good morning, ladies," he blushed.

"Where's Roland?" asked the blonde one. He had learned her name was Nerissa.

"Oh," he said with surprise. He did not realize they were never told he had left.

"Yes, is he coming?" asked the one called Ianthe.

"I'm sorry to be the one to tell you this, but he's gone," he answered.

The red-haired one, Maraja, furrowed her brow. "Gone where?"

"Back home, to the realm of the gods," he explained. "He left over a month ago."

Their eyes went wide with shock, then they let out an ear-piercing, mournful wail. Rhydian covered his ears, but could not block it out completely. They were behaving as if he had died. The will-o-wisps had all fled at the sound of their unified cry.

"Ladies, please," he shouted over their cries.

His ears were ringing and his head hurt by the time they had calmed down to soft sobs.

"Why would he leave?" Ianthe sniffled.

"He had no choice. His mother commanded it," he said. He purposefully left out why. Roland had warned him of their jealous nature and dislike of Kezia.

"Why are you here, Rhydian?" asked Maraja, with an air of suspicion.

He took a moment before responding. "We need your help," he implored, his voice tinged with desperation. "My mother and I are struggling without my father. Can you provide us with your healing tears one last time?"

The mermaids exchanged glances, their shimmering forms reflecting the light of the will-o-wisps that had returned. They circled like sharks, and Rhydian was glad he did not get into the pool with them. Finally, the eldest of them swam forward, her voice harsh.

"Why should we help? You are Roland's son, but you are also hers," Maraja hissed.

"Please," he pleaded. "My father wouldn't want us to suffer in his absence."

The circling continued as they considered his request. Then, after a few agonizing moments, they swam back to the edge of the pool, and Maraja spoke again.

"We will help you, Rhydian, but only this once." She took the bottles from him.

With a graceful motion, they sang, their haunting melody filling the air. As their song reached its crescendo, tears flowed down their cheeks, collected into the glass bottles. Once full, they handed them back to Rhydian, their expressions sad. After that, they swam off before he could thank them.

Grateful beyond words, Rhydian corked the bottles and hurried back to the house to get started on the tincture. When he was done, he went in search of his mother. He found her still in her room, sitting by the window, lost in thought. He approached her with the mermaid tears tincture, but she did not notice him. At least she was out of bed.

"Mother," he said softly, taking her hand. "I brought something for you."

"Hm?" she murmured, still not looking at him. "Just put it on the table. I'll eat it later."

His heart broke seeing her like that. "It's not food, mother," he said, kneeling next to her.

Finally, she turned to him, her beautiful, bright gray eyes now dull and lifeless.

He placed the small bottle in her hands. "It's father's tincture for you."

She perked up at that, looking down at the bottle.

"Please, drink it. You'll feel better once you do," he tried.

She pushed the bottle away. "I don't want it. I need Roland, not some temporary magical solution." She turned away from him to stare out the window again.

"Mother, please. I need you. Do it for me," he begged, agony in his voice.

Again, she turned to him, frowning when she saw how distraught he was. She reached out and gently touched his face. "I'm so sorry, my darling. I forgot you can feel my pain, too."

He leaned into the warmth of her hand, briefly closing his eyes to stop the tears. When he opened them again, she was smiling weakly at him. She took the bottle from him, uncorked it, and drank its contents. Then she shut her eyes and breathed in deeply, a brighter smile warming her features. She sat the empty bottle down and pulled him into her embrace. It was then that he broke down for the first time since his father left. Softly, she cooed and rubbed his back as he cried for a man he was finally getting to know.

They sat like that, her holding and rocking him for what felt like hours.

She pulled him from her, a gentle smile on her face. "Perhaps you should have a bottle yourself?"

He nodded, wiping away an errant tear. "I will, but I wanted to take care of you first. And you shouldn't have the same need for it as you did father's. I'm afraid it's not as strong, but it will help you still."

"Thank you. Maybe we could take a walk around the garden and talk about your father later?"

"Yes, I would like that," he agreed.

"Good," she smiled. "For now, let's get something to eat. I'm absolutely famished."

Again, he nodded, getting up. He helped her to her feet, and they walked downstairs together. She was still feeling a little weak, so he had to hold on to her as they descended the stairs.

After lunch, they took a walk in the garden. He had taken the tincture, and they laughed as they shared stories of their time with Roland. He even told her about how he helped him with his incubus nature. She paled before bursting into a laughing fit. They continued their walk, stopping at one of the stone benches so she could rest a bit, before going back in to play a game of cards. Something they both enjoyed that Roland never got the hang of. He was bonding with his mother again, and it brought him so much joy and lessened the pain of not having his father around. At least for now.

# CHAPTER 34

K ezia sighed as she sank into Roland's office chair, his familiar scent still lingering in the room. It already felt like a lifetime since she had heard his voice, held his hand, or seen his scruffy face. She missed him terribly. Sitting in his office was her way of feeling close to him, of keeping his memory alive in the small, everyday moments. Rhydian could have taken over the space, but chose not to. It was his father's office. He would make his own.

She smiled and blushed when she looked over at the sofa in the room. They had made love many times on it. Though it was not the most comfortable place they had done it, the memories still warmed her heart, among other things. She once again swallowed her lust.

As she sorted through the papers on his desk, her fingers brushed against a worn leather-bound journal. It was a simple-looking thing. With its plain black covering. She hesitated for a moment, then carefully opened its cover. Roland's neat, distinctive handwriting filled the pages. It did not take long for her to realize that this was his most private record. She was not aware he kept such a thing, but it explained why he was always in his office when he was not with her or consoling souls.

Her eyes welled up as she read the entry he wrote last. She could almost hear his voice speaking the words aloud as she read.

30th of May 1918

The weight of my promise to Vala has been ever-present on my mind. My decision to fulfill this promise has been challenging. to say the least. I still can't believe my brother. my twin. could have wronged me so. He took my first love from me. And for what? Petty jealousy? Now he wants to take Kezia. my heart and soul. away from me as well as our only son. And after he had already stolen and murdered our daughter.

I don't understand what I could have done to upset my brother in such a way that he would do so much evil. He was so adamant about maintaining the natural order of things when we were in the celestial realm. Now, he seeks revenge for some imagined slight.

When Vala possessed Kezia's body, it broke me. I still refused to agree to killing my brother, but I wanted Kezia back. I needed her, and I would do anything to bring her back to me, but killing my brother was out of the question. When Lux told me that our little girl was alive, in Hungary of all places, I was elated. I wanted to go after her, but I feared leaving Kezia and Rhydian without my protection. But after Vala told me that Ozmir had taken my daughter's body and destroyed her soul, I finally agreed to Vala's terms. I wholeheartedly regret not acting sooner to save my daughter's life. There was so much I didn't know, and now I'll never get the chance to know her. Especially when I had already buggered things with her brother. If I could do things over. I would have agreed to do Vala's bidding sooner. But Ozmir is—was my brother.

After that, I agreed to kill my brother to save the rest of my family. But that wasn't all. Vala made me promise to return to the celestial realm once it was done. I had to remember that I was doing it for my family, but I couldn't bring myself to tell anyone. Not even Lux or Nox.

I should have been a better father to Rhydian, but I was so in my head with Kezia being in a coma that I couldn't be there for him like he needed. I am grateful for the time I did have raising him and for reconnecting with him now. Sometimes I wonder if I had gotten to Kezia sooner. The first time we actually met, things might have been different. I would have married her sooner, and we could have had our family then.

I know there's no point in dwelling on what could have been or what I could have done differently, but no matter what the outcome of my fight with Ozmir, I wouldn't change my decisions. Killing Ozzy would feel like severing a part of myself, despite his actions. However, my family's safety and wellbeing are more important. I love my wife and son so much that I would see this world drown to ensure their survival.

My only hope is that my family knows how much they mean to me. I will spend what time I have left in the mortal realm showing them that they mean everything and more. If there was anything I could do to get out of my deal with Vala without hurting my family, I would, but a vow made to a goddess is difficult to break.

When the time comes, and Ozmir is dead, I will have to leave my beloved family to return to the one that I abandoned centuries ago. This will be my punishment for all the lives I had taken so long ago and the one I plan to take. I do this to see my Kezia smile again and to hold her in my arms once more.

-Roland

Tears streamed down Kezia's face as she closed the journal. It was his last entry. Roland had shouldered such an immense burden to bring her back. He must have felt so alone. She clutched the journal to her chest, feeling an overwhelming need to be with him. The journal was all she had left of his thoughts and feelings, and she did not know if he would ever return to her and their son. There was no mention of it, and he was punishing himself for his past misdeeds. It left her wondering if Vala would do the same. Would her love be stripped of his godhood and be made mortal as his brother was?

She got up, still holding on tight to the journal, and laid down on the sofa. She curled into a ball around the leather tome of her husband's words and memories, and cried herself to sleep.

# CHAPTER 35

The celestial realm was a place of ethereal beauty, with its ivory towers and lush greenery, but to Roland, it felt cold and distant. Vala's punishment weighed heavily on him, as she had forbidden him from checking on his family. He was lucky that it was as far as the punishment went. He should have been made Fallen, but since he had blood bound himself to mortals, making him Fallen would kill them as his life was still linked to theirs. His continuance of his godly duties while in the mortal realm also helped lessen his punishment. It was a cruel twist of fate, one that left him sullen and grumpy as he performed his duties as a god.

Each day, he carried out his tasks with a heavy heart. His once purposed actions now felt hollow, like a meaningless chore to be done. He found some solace, if only in his interactions with the souls he guided into the afterlife. Their varied reactions to his confessions offered a fleeting connection to the world he had been torn from.

One such day, Roland stood by the eternal river that served as a passage to the afterlife. The shimmering waters reflected the starlight, casting an otherworldly glow on the souls gathered there. He had a similar setup to the table in his Gray room back in the mortal realm. It stood on the side of the river, beckoning the company of the next soul. Sadly, he had no calming tea to offer them.

As he prepared to see off the soul of an elderly woman with kind eyes and a gentle smile, he found himself confiding in the old girl.

"You must miss them terribly," the woman said, her voice full of sympathy.

"I do," Roland replied, his tone somber. "Every moment without them is a reminder of what I've lost."

The woman reached out, her translucent hand brushing against his. "I hope you find peace, and may your loved ones feel your presence, even from afar."

Roland nodded, a faint smile touching his lips as he watched her cross the river, disappearing into the light. He wondered how she drowned. Perhaps he should have asked before letting her go.

Not all souls were understanding. Some showed indifference, their own burdens overshadowing any sympathy they might have felt for him. A gruff man with a stern expression sat down next, his demeanor almost belligerent.

"It's not my concern," the man said flatly. "I have my own troubles to worry about."

Roland felt a pang of frustration. He had only asked if the man had a family he was leaving behind and how he missed his, but he remained composed. "We all have our struggles," he said, his gaze fixed on the river. "Even those who are supposed to be divine."

The man shrugged, offering no further words as he crossed the river and plummeted to the underworld, leaving Roland to his thoughts. Roland was sure someone murdered the man, and he likely deserved it.

There were those who felt awkward, unsure of how to respond to a god's vulnerability. A young woman with wide eyes and a nervous smile hesitated before speaking.

"I never imagined a god could feel such pain," she admitted, shifting uncomfortably in her seat.

"We all have our battles," Roland said softly, "and sometimes the ones fought inside are the hardest of all."

The young woman nodded, her expression thoughtful as she made her way across the river, her spirit at ease.

As the night deepened and the stars above offered no solace, Roland wandered to a quiet corner of the celestial realm. The distant light reminded him of the separation between the divine and mortal worlds. His heart ached with longing for his wife and son, the love he held for them burning like the eternal flame he had extinguished in his brother.

He found himself standing on the edge of the celestial realm, looking down at the world he had fought to remain a part of.

"I will find my way back to you, Kezia," he whispered to the wind, his eyes filled with tears and determination. "No matter how long it takes."

With his quiet vow in his heart, he turned back to his duties. Despite the pain of his separation from his family, he clung to the belief that one day, he would be reunited with them, and he could leave the celestial realm behind once and for all.

# CHAPTER 36

Kezia sat in Roland's office, the leather-bound journal open in her lap. Though she had taken the mermaid tears tincture, she still felt lonely without her husband. Even when she was angry with him, she knew he would always be there. Being in his office and reading his journal somehow made her feel close to him again. He spoke freely, and it was like she was getting to know him all over again.

There were entries of when they first met and how he truly felt about her. His private thoughts were so intimate, and somewhat infuriating since he never bothered to share these feelings with her, but his actions usually made up for it. There were even times that she laughed because her libido had overwhelmed and frightened him so much that he had to hide from her.

"Mother?" came a soft, deep voice, and a light knock on the door.

"Hm? Oh, Rhydian!" she beamed.

"Are you all right?" he asked worriedly. "You weren't at dinner last night or at lunch today."

She continued to smile at him. "I'm fine, my darling. Lynnox was kind enough to bring me something earlier. Did you need something?"

"No," he said, shaking his head. "I just wanted to check on you."

She closed the journal and patted the seat beside her on the sofa. "Why don't you tell me how you and Dorian are doing? How's the business?"

He happily took the seat next to her and smiled. "Things are going well, actually. Dorian has been a big help. I don't know the first thing about plants," he admitted.

"Neither did your father. Not at first, anyway," she laughed.

He furrowed his brow at her. "I thought he was an apothecary before you two met."

"He was," she started. "But I've been reading his journal." She held up the enormous book with both hands.

"Ah, I see. So that's why I haven't seen you," he smiled. "Any interesting secrets?"

"Many!" she said in a scandalized tone, her eyes wide.

"Really? Like what?" he asked curiously.

She laughed. "Perhaps I'll share them with you when you're older," she grinned.

He chuckled and gave her a light kiss on the cheek before getting up. "Well, I see you're in good spirits, at least. I'll leave you to your reading."

"Thank you," she said, her voice soft and warm.

"Just don't hide in here. It makes me worry."

She nodded, then opened the journal to a random page. She waved him off as he left before going back to her reading.

15th of April 1912

The days blend together in a haze of routine and longing. Kezia remains in a coma. and our home has been shrouded in quiet grief ever since. It's hard to put into words the pain I feel watching her lie there. lifeless yet alive. I visit her bedside daily. holding her hand and telling her stories of the world that continues to turn without her.

Rhydian is ten now. a bright young man with a thirst for knowledge and a spirit that shines with a light I know he didn't get from me. It's heartbreaking that he's never known his mother—never heard her laugh. felt her embrace or seen the sparkle in her eyes. He only knows her through my stories and the few faded photographs we have.

I see so much of Kezia in him. Every smile, every inquisitive glance, every passionate pursuit. It's as if she lives on in him. Helping him navigate life without her is challenging, and I'm grateful to Nox for all her help with him.

Despite my best efforts, I know I've been distant. The weight of my responsibilities and the hollowness I feel without my love has created a barrier between me and our son. He has taken my cello, and I'm sure he thinks I haven't noticed, but I stopped playing it long ago. He is welcomed to it if it makes him happy.

Rhydian has his moments of frustration and anger, and Nox encourages him to express those feelings. I want him *to feel supported. to know that he's not alone in his journey into manhood. but I find it hard to bring myself to be near him now. He looks so much like his mother. and I can't bear it.*

*In my quiet moments. when the house is still. I allow myself to mourn the life we could've had together. I miss Kezia more than words can convey. and I'm lost without her. I hold on to the hope that one day she'll wake and see the remarkable young man our son is becoming without us.*

*-Roland*

Her heart broke at his words. She had read every entry multiple times, each word a lifeline to the man she loved and missed so dearly, but some entries made her sad. Some made her angry. How could he just refuse to raise their son like that? No wonder it was so easy for Rhydian to go on without him.

Not all the entries upset her, but the more she read, the more vivid her dreams of him became. It was as if Roland was visiting her in the night, his presence so real that she could almost feel his touch. The dreams were not just figments of her imagination. They were intense and consuming. She would wake up in a haze, her body aching and longing. The dreams were so lifelike that she saw Roland everywhere—in the hallways, in the garden, and especially in their bedroom. He was like a specter haunting her. His absence was a constant ache, and her desire for him grew stronger with each passing day. All because she kept reading his journal. It was as if it linked them outside of their blood bond. Like he had returned to her.

Her longing was so powerful that it affected the entire household. The air was thick with an unspoken tension, a palpable energy that emanated from her. Her lust, born from the vivid dreams and the deep love she still held for Roland, seeped into every corner of the mansion. The servants whispered about the strange atmosphere, feeling the effects of her powerful emotions.

Each night, she would lie in bed, clutching Roland's journal to her chest, and let the dreams wash over her. In those moments, he was with her, and the world felt right again. Despite the overwhelming desire, Kezia refused to take lovers to her bed. Her heart and body belonged to Roland, and she could not bring herself to seek comfort in the arms of another. She could feel Rhydian's concern for her, but she ignored it. She was fine so long as she had Roland's journal.

As the days turned into weeks, Kezia became more withdrawn again. Soon, she barely ate and would either stay in bed or she would lock herself in Roland's office. Her lust spells created rampant mating in the house that got so bad that many left, refusing to come back until things were better. But that was just one more thing going on that she did not care about.

# CHAPTER 37

Roland felt isolated in the celestial realm, despite being surrounded by divine beauty and family. He had his other siblings, aunts, uncles, and cousins there, but they wanted little to do with him. They thought he had spent too much time with mortals, and it made him soft in their minds. He had also bound himself to a mortal and spawned demigods, something that just was not done. They did not seek to harm Rhydian, but they would never allow him among them. Roland was starting to remember why he left in the first place and why his brother went mad.

As he freely flew around in his full dragon form, he was consumed by thoughts of his mortal family, and their absence never dulled in his heart. His wings beat the sky, his black scales shimmering with iridescent blues like finely polished labradorite in the light of the morning sun. He did his best not to let his melancholy get the better of him, and flying above the heavens often helped with that. Recently, he had felt intense sadness and lust emanating from Kezia, and he felt Rhydian's worry for her. Her energy was growing weaker, and it gave him cause for concern as well.

He knew she would refuse to take others to their bed, which he was fine with, but she could feed in other ways to sustain herself. Roland feared that her refusal to feed was not only affecting her health, but also pushing her closer to losing control. He knew if she lost control, the consequences would be dire for her and for Rhydian.

Vala had bound his ability to fast travel to prevent him from coming and going as he pleased, and he was forbidden from using the celestial gates. Resolved to help her, Roland thought of sneaking away from his duties to visit her, regardless of Vala's strict prohibition. The promise he had made to his mother to leave his family behind felt like a shackle around his heart. He would risk whatever punishment he would get for disobeying her.

One night, under the cover of darkness, Roland moved quietly through the celestial realm in his human guise. He planned his route to the main gates carefully, avoiding the watchful eyes of his fellow gods and goddesses. His heart pounded in his ears, knowing what he was about to do could have severe consequences. And not all gods slept.

"Zaven?" came the voice of Rah'ja, his eastern cousin. "What are you doing skulking around at this hour?"

"Oh, I couldn't sleep. So I thought I would take a walk to tire myself out," he answered, a nervous smile on his face.

Rah'ja eyed him with some suspicion, then his expression softened. "I see having a pulse has made things hard for you."

"It has," he said solemnly.

"Well," he started, "don't stray too far to the edge of the realm. You know Vala has eyes everywhere," he warned, putting a hand on Roland's shoulder.

"I am aware," he sighed.

Rah'ja bowed his head, then walked off after giving Roland a knowing look. Roland let out a breath of relief before continuing on his path.

As he neared the boundary gates that separated the celestial and mortal realms, he felt a sudden, chilling presence. He turned to see two of Vala's familiars— spectral creatures he had never seen before—emerged from the shadows. Their eyes glowed with a piercing light, and their forms shifted and flickered like the remnants of a forgotten nightmare.

"Zaven," one spoke, its voice echoing with an otherworldly resonance. "You know Vala's command. You are forbidden from crossing into the mortal realm."

Roland's heart sank, but he tried to maintain his composure. "I just need to see my wife," he pleaded, his voice filled with desperation. "Kezia is getting weaker, and I'm afraid she'll lose control. Please, let me help her."

The familiars' eyes did not waver, their expressions remaining stern and impassive. "Vala's decree is absolute. You must return to your quarters," the other said.

Anger and frustration welled up within Roland, but he knew there was no point in arguing. His emotions would not sway the familiars. With his hands in tight fists at his sides, he reluctantly walked away.

As he walked back to his quarters, he felt the all too familiar ache of longing for his wife. The knowledge that she was struggling and that he could do nothing about it tormented him. He vowed to find another way to reach her, to provide the support she needed, and to ensure the demon within her remained dormant.

In the days that followed, Roland redoubled his efforts in his divine tasks, hoping to appease Vala and earn a reprieve that would allow him to visit his family. The souls he guided to the afterlife became his confidants, sharing in his sorrow and offering words of encouragement.

Every night, he lay awake thinking of his family. He did his best to remain cheerful, hoping Kezia would feel it and be happy, too, but her melancholy only grew worse. He needed to reach her before it was too late. The order of extermination had laxed over the years since Rhydian had been born, but still he worried for them. Though she was no longer an assassin, she was still dangerous. He prayed that those around her found a way to help her soon.

When he managed to fall asleep, the possibility of his family being hunted and killed plagued his dreams. And there was not a damn thing he could do.

# CHAPTER 38

Rhydian sighed as he walked through the mansion, his steps heavy with worry. It had been months, nearly a year, since his father had gone. He went in search of his mother and found that she was not in her room. Once again, he found her in his father's office, her nose buried in the thick leather journal she always kept with her. It had become a daily ritual, a way for her to feel close to him. He thought of boarding up the room or repurposing it to keep her out of it, but he knew that would do no good.

"Mother," he called softly, entering the room.

Kezia looked up, her eyes filled with a mix of longing and weariness. She weakly smiled at him, but the pain in her gaze was unmistakable.

"How are you feeling today?" he asked, but he could see for himself.

She had dark circles around her eyes and she was barely more than skin and bones.

"I swear, I can see him and feel him still," she said, clutching the journal to her chest with fear in her eyes. She did not want him to take it.

Rhydian's heart broke at her words. He had heard them countless times, each repetition a reminder of her lasting grief. He had tried to take the book from her once before, but it did not end well. She nearly tore the house apart looking for it, screaming and crying as she did so. He gave it back, and she immediately calmed down. Even Ariel was at a loss for what to do with her. She refused to feed off of him.

Deciding that something needed to be done, Rhydian set off to seek the help of the mermaids once more. He went to the secluded grotto, finding its path overgrown and wild; however, his hopes were dashed when he reached the pool. The mermaids were gone, their once vibrant home now empty and silent. The water was still, and even the will-o-wisps had left. Despair weighed heavily on his shoulders as he returned to the mansion, unsure of what to do next.

Back at the estate, Rhydian sought Lynnox. He found her cleaning the second-floor parlor room, meticulously arranging the shelves. Her blue feline eyes looked up to meet his as he approached.

"Lady Lynnox, I need your help," he began, his voice tinged with exhaustion and desperation.

"What is it, love?" she asked in a worried tone.

"The mermaids are gone, and mother is still so broken and depressed. I fear she isn't feeding enough, and I don't know what to do."

Lynnox sighed, her expression softening. "Rhydian, yer mum is havin' a rough go of things right now. She needs to let Zaven go, and that takes time. Ya can't force her to move on. They have too much love and history together for it to be that easy."

"But she's wasting away," he argued, his frustration building. "I can't just stand by and watch her suffer."

Lynnox placed a comforting hand on Rhydian's arm, her voice gentle yet firm. "She needs to find her own way through this. All ya can do is be there for her and encourage her to take care of herself. She'll need to feed eventually, but pushin' her now might do more harm than good."

Rhydian nodded reluctantly, his worry pressing down on him. "I hate seeing her like this," he admitted, his voice barely above a whisper.

"We all do, love," she replied softly. "But she's stronger than ya think, and she has ya by her side. That counts for somethin'."

Again, he nodded, but he was not so sure that his mother was as strong as Lynnox thought. Still, he would try to give her the time she needed, making sure that he was close should she need him.

Wanting to help in any way possible, Rhydian went back to his mother, who was still engrossed in his father's journal. He sat beside her, reaching out to take her hand. "Mother, I love you, but I need you here with me, present and healthy. I know you miss father, and so do I, but we have to take care of each other."

Kezia looked at him, her eyes glistening with tears. She squeezed his hand, a small gesture of acknowledgement. "I know, but it's just so hard to let him go."

"We don't have to let go entirely," he said gently. "We can keep his memory alive in our hearts, but we need to live our lives, too. He wouldn't want us to be consumed by grief."

Kezia nodded. "Thank you, my darling. I'll try." She went back to her reading.

He leaned in and kissed her forehead, his heart hopeful. They were in this together, and he would do everything in his power to support her. He refused to let her shut him out like Roland had for so many years. Healing her heart would take time, but first, he needed to get that book away from her for good.

"Mother?"

"Hm? Yes, my darling?" she answered, still reading.

"May I have father's journal?" he asked softly, reaching for the book.

She quickly closed it and held it tight to her chest, her eyes wide in fear again. "No," she blurted out, her tone harsh. Her eyes flashed red for a moment, but went back to normal.

"Mother, please," he pleaded, pulling his hands back. "You don't need it."

"You don't know what I need," she growled.

"But you're barely eating, and you're sleeping so much. Just let me have it for a little while," he tried, reaching out again.

"I said no," she hissed, getting up.

He could hear the low rumble of a growl as she backed away from him. His heart broke at the sight of her. She was so frail that she could barely stand on her own. He could easily take the book away, but he knew she would never forgive him for it, and he would lose her completely. She had to be willing to give it up.

"I won't take it from you," he said in a cautious tone.

"Then leave," she ordered, still defensive.

"Mother—"

"I said get out!" she commanded.

Rhydian's eyes went wide in shock, his mouth gaped open. She trembled with anger, resembling a confronted addict, but she had never yelled at him before. Lynnox was right. She was going to need time to let go on her own. He could not force it.

He sighed as he got up. Giving her one last mournful look, he left, shutting the door behind him. A dark thought crossed his mind as he leaned against the door. He might as well be an orphan. Both his parents were lost to him now.

# CHAPTER 39

T he lamplight flickered softly in the quiet room as Kezia turned the delicate pages of the worn journal. Her fingertips glided over the words, and though they were not her own, they carried a weight that settled heavily in her chest. Roland's handwriting—firm yet occasionally wavering—reflected the man himself: strong, but burdened by unseen cracks. As she read, Roland's guilt bled through the ink.

30th of April 1918

It's Kezia's birthday today, but still, she sleeps. Rhydian's was last month. Rhydian carries both of our blood. Mine and hers. This has always been at the forefront of my mind, yet I fear I've failed him more than I ever thought possible. How can I guide a boy whose very existence is a battle between worlds—one foot in light, the other in shadow? He deserves better, someone wiser, more patient. Someone like Caelum. If only he were here, perhaps he would know how to reach Rhydian, to temper the storm that rages inside him.

I see his mother in him all the time. Not just her face, but her nature—the allure, the intensity. It terrifies me., His incubus side could be as dangerous as hers ever was, perhaps more so, amplified by the power coursing through him as a demigod. How do I protect him from himself when I can't even protect him from my blood within him?

It shames me to admit this, but I think I've driven him away. He doesn't use his hydrokinesis anymore, and I blame myself for it. I never truly taught him to wield it—not in its full potential, not in the way he deserved. When he was little, he would spend hours by the lake, coaxing the water into currents and shapes that danced like they were alive. I remember the way my chest swelled with pride watching him. He was so full of determination, so, alive.

Now? He seeks counsel from Ariel and Luxor instead of me. Maybe he sees me as weak, or worse, irrelevant. I try not to let that bitterness take hold, but it lingers, festering. I should be proud that he's sought out wisdom where I could not provide it. but it only reminds me of my shortcomings. My shame is a heavy chain. and I don't know how to break free of it.

There are moments I wonder if it's too late. Too late to fix what I've broken. Too late to be the father he needs. But there's a small. stubborn part of me that hopes-hopes that there's still a way forward. For him. and for me.

-Roland

The description of Rhydian's hydrokinesis, once a source of pride and joy, now reduced to a memory, painted a stark contrast between the past and the present. Kezia could almost see the boy in her mind—Rhydian, with his youthful determination, standing by a serene lake, coaxing water to dance at his fingertips. The way Roland described it, there was awe in his eyes back then, a father's pride swelling within him. And now? That pride was hollow, replaced by the ache of shame.

The mention of Rhydian's incubus nature made Kezia's breath catch. The words seemed to shimmer on the page, almost alive with unspoken fear. Roland's concern was not just for the boy's safety but for the destruction his untamed powers could unleash. There was a certain fragility in his admission of missing Caelum, a loneliness

Kezia understood all too well. She imagined Roland, isolated in his struggles, yearning for a companion who could share the weight of it all.

Her hands trembled slightly as she absorbed the final lines, the part about Rhydian seeking counsel from Ariel and Luxor instead of his father. Roland's shame hung heavily in the air, and Kezia felt it as though it were her own. She closed the journal gently; her gaze lingering on the leather cover.

Kezia exhaled slowly, her mind churning. This entry was not just a window into Roland's thoughts—it was a mirror of Rhydian's struggles. It was clear that Roland's regrets had shaped their fractured bond. She was at a loss for what to do about any of it. Roland was no longer there. She could not help them fix their bond to make it better. Though Rhydian had said he had forgiven his father, she still felt as though there was a part of him that still resented Roland for his neglect over the years. Now she felt bad for snapping at him earlier. She would put the journal away and make amends with him.

With a sigh, she tucked the book under her arm and got up. She was tired, and it was late. When she swayed slightly, she realized she had forgotten to feed again. It normally would not have bothered her, but she had suddenly felt so weak… and so very hungry. She collapsed to the floor, and the room swirled into an abyss of black.

# CHAPTER 40

He followed the trail of bodies to find her…

It was two days before anyone had noticed she was missing, but the husk of a male servant behind the hedges on the newly restored front lawn had given them a reason to look for her. Then the reports of demon attacks in the city came in. She had left in the night.

It was too dangerous for Rhydian; she was not in her right mind and would attack him. No one wanted him to have to fight his own mother, and Ariel's job was to protect the grounds with his pack. Luxor received the task of finding her and bringing her back safely. Two more days went by before he finally picked up her trail. The hour was late when he did. She was being smart and staying hidden during the day, only coming out at night to feed.

The people in town did not come out at night for fear of being attacked. Even those that called themselves demon hunters were too frightened to venture out. Only drunks and vagrants dared to go out alone.

From a safe distance, he watched her as she sat on top of her latest victim. He could have stopped her. He wanted to, but the man was already too far gone, and his death would be painless. At least, he hoped it would be. Death buried deep in the cunt of a beautiful woman seemed much more appealing than having his throat ripped out. Which would have happened if he interrupted them.

So, he waited.

As she reached climax, her wings and tail shot out of her. She threw her head back, her expression one of sheer bliss as the ethereal light of his life essence filled her. It made her whole, and she looked young and healthy again. He swore under his breath. She would not come easily.

She removed herself from the husk, her body silhouetted in the moon's light as she stretched. It was both a beautiful and frightening sight to behold. He was glad he was not blood bound to her husband as she was. He would certainly kill him for looking at his wife with such lust in his eyes. Then again, she had that effect on everyone.

"Why don't you come out, Luxor," she purred. "I know you're there. Naughty kitty." She had a wide smile on her face, her fangs bared.

He stepped out into the pale light, his form sleek and graceful. "You need to come home, my Lady. It's not safe for you out here."

She laughed wickedly. "I'm not the one who isn't safe, and I'm having so much fun."

"Kezia, please. Don't make me hurt you," he pleaded. "Zaven wouldn't be happy with me if anything bad happened to you."

She frowned at that. "Well, he isn't here, is he?"

He sighed. "No, I suppose he isn't," he agreed, readying himself to attack.

With a swift motion, Luxor lunged forward, his claws out. Kezia's movements were fluid, almost graceful, as she counterattacked. She dodged another fierce blow from Luxor, her quick reflexes saving her from harm. With a spin, she aimed a strike at Luxor's side, only for him to deflect her kick with a quick block that pushed her back a fair distance.

Kezia stood poised with predatory grace, her eyes glowing a deadly red. Luxor appeared deceptively calm. His eyes, slitted, gleamed with a dangerous intensity. This time, Kezia was the first to move. With a burst of supernatural speed, she lunged at him; her nails extended into sharp claws. Luxor matched her agility, dodging to the side with a fluid motion, his hand swiping with razor-sharp precision. He had barely missed her.

Kezia's agility allowed for rapid, high kicks aimed at Luxor's head, to which he responded with equally fast, low sweeps at her legs, trying to unbalance her. She was not moving like someone who had been in a coma for nearly two decades, and he was sure she was actively trying to kill him.

They moved in perfect harmony, each sensing the other's next move in a deadly ballet. His hands and feet were as fast as lightning, blocking and countering her strikes with a nimbleness only a demonic cat could possess.

With a fierce snarl, she summoned her full powers, her eyes glowing brighter as she attempted to drain his life force. She reached for him, her touch filled with an energy-sapping chill. Well, that was a new trick. But ever the agile feline, he twisted away just in time, his own demonic aura flaring to life. He retaliated by pouncing on her, his strength and speed overwhelming her as he propelled her backwards.

They tumbled across the ground, each struggling for dominance. Kezia's strength, fueled by her dark nature, was formidable, but his lithe form and superior reflexes allowed him to evade her attacks while delivering his own punishing blows. He did his best not to hurt her too badly, but she was not making it easy for him.

Kezia's wings unfurled from her back, and she took to the air, gaining an advantage with her aerial attacks. Luxor, unphased, dodged her when she swooped down at him. When she was back in the air, he leapt high with a grace only a Nakaru could achieve, meeting her mid-air. Their bodies collided with an impact that reverberated through them.

As the fight wore on, neither showed signs of tiring. Each attack was met with a counter, each move calculated with deadly precision. She struck out at him with the end of her barbed tail, slicing into his side and leaving a deep gash. He cursed aloud; he had forgotten about her tail. Smiling, she struck out with it a second time, aiming for his chest, as she swiped with her claws.

"If I didn't know any better, I'd say you were trying to kill me, milady."

A slow smile formed on her face. "Perhaps I am."

He caught her tail while avoiding her claws and ripped the deadly appendage from her back.

She let out a demonic screech, leaping back, then tried to take to the air once more. However, without her tail, she was off balance and came crashing back down immediately. She hissed as she staggered back to her feet. His agility and feline reflexes were winning out despite his injury. Even with her blood lust, Kezia found herself slowly losing ground. Especially now that her aerial advantage was gone. His movements were a ballet of deadly elegance, his demonic aura pulsing with power.

With a final, powerful leap, he pounced on her, pinning her to the ground. She struggled beneath him, her eyes blazing with rage, but his strength was overwhelming.

Luxor's eyes glowed with a predatory triumph as he delivered a swift, precise strike to her temple, rendering her unconscious. She slumped against the cold ground, her wings limp and her form still.

The once deafening sounds of their battle faded into the night, replaced by the quiet rustle of the wind across the city. Luxor rolled off of her, his chest heaving with exertion. He held his still bleeding side; the wound was deep, but already healing. She was going to be pissed at him for ripping out her tail, but he could live with that. Though he hoped it grew back. If Zaven ever returned, he would kill him for mutilating his wife. Even if it was in self-defense.

He slowly rose to his feet, looking down at Kezia, his eyes never leaving her body. His eyes went wide briefly, and he blushed, swallowing hard. She was still very naked. With an exasperated sigh, he carefully lifted her in his arms, mindful of where his hands were, and vanished in a puff of smoke.

# CHAPTER 41

ezia's eyes fluttered open to the dim glow of a soft light. Her surroundings were unfamiliar, and a dull throbbing ache pulsed through her head. When she attempted to move, she realized her wrists and ankles were bound with heavy chains. Her chest heaved as she struggled to take in air, and there was a high-pitched ringing in her ears as she fought against the chains. Before she could scream, a voice cut through her panic.

"Yer finally awake," Lynnox said, her tone a mix of relief and wariness. She appeared at her side, her blue eyes filled with concern.

Kezia struggled to sit up, her mind a fog of confusion. "What happened? Where am I?"

Lynnox sat beside her, her expression softening. "Ya don't remember? Lux... he went out to fetch ya. He brought ya home to recover." She paused, gauging her reaction. "Ya were outta control, love. We couldn't let ya hurt anyone else. Yer in the dungeon for now. We didn't want Rhydian to see ya like ya were."

The memories slowly trickled back, and Kezia's breath caught in her throat. She felt the weight of her actions press down on her, and tears welled up in her eyes. It was like she was a spectator in her own body. She had killed so many in just a few days. And she hurt Luxor. "I... I didn't mean to," she choked out. "I couldn't control myself."

Lynnox placed a reassuring hand on her shoulder. "I know. Somethin' has to change, poppet. Ya need to feed regularly if ya don't wanna lose control again."

Kezia's gaze fell, her world crumbling. "I don't know how to fix this," she cried. "I know I can't keep living like this, but I miss him so much."

"I know ya do, love, but he's gone and we don't know if he'll ever come back. Ya have yer son to think about, and the boy needs his mum," she fussed lightly.

"Yes, my son needs me. He's all I have left of my love. I must take care of him."

Lynnox nodded. "And yerself," she added. "Promise me ya will keep yerself fed. Ya can't afford another rampage, not with him dependin' on ya. We can keep the authorities away for now, but their fear of Zaven isn't what it used to be," she explained.

With a heavy heart, Kezia nodded. "I understand. I promise to keep myself fed, so this doesn't happen again."

Lynnox reached into the pocket of her apron and pulled out a set of large, old keys.

"And one more thing," Kezia started, her voice unsteady. "Put Roland's journal away. Somewhere I can't find it."

Lynnox furrowed her brow but agreed. "If that's what ya need." She unlocked the chains, setting Kezia free. "Just don't go destroyin' the house again lookin' for it."

Kezia rubbed her wrists, feeling the weight of her promise settle over her. As she stood up, she took a deep breath, vowing to control the darkness within her.

She reached her hand out to Kezia. "C'mon, love, I'll get a hot bath ready for ya and make ya somethin' to eat."

"All right," Kezia murmured, taking Lynnox's hand.

Lynnox smiled up at her as they walked through the large, heavy metal door. It was then that Kezia realized where they were. She fell to her knees and broke down in tears. She could hear Lynnox making soft shushing noises as she gently rubbed her back. Everything was a reminder of Roland and their story together. She needed to get away for a while until she felt better. Rhydian would understand. He might even join her, but she could no longer let her grief destroy her life. And she could not do to Rhydian what Roland had. She would not abandon him a second time.

The gondolas glided serenely along the Venetian canals as Kezia and Rhydian stepped off the boat and onto the cobblestone streets. The city was bathed in the soft light of early afternoon, its charm offering a temporary escape from their grief.

Kezia kept a firm grip on Rhydian's hand, his long fingers wrapped around hers. The journey to Venice was meant to aid their healing, allowing them to find solace in the city's timeless beauty and rich history following her fight with Luxor and the loss of Roland.

They wandered through the narrow alleyways, taking in the splendor of the Renaissance architecture and the vibrant market places. Rhydian's eyes were wide with wonder as he marveled at the intricate masks displayed in shop windows and the musicians playing soulful melodies in the piazzas.

"Mother, can we get some gelato?" he asked, his voice hopeful.

Kezia smiled, her heartwarming at the sight of her son's excitement. It was as if he were a child again. "Of course, my darling," she replied, leading him to a nearby gelateria.

Together, they savored the sweet, creamy treat, finding a momentary reprieve from their sorrow.

As they continued their stroll, Kezia could not help but feel a pang of longing for her husband. His absence was a constant ache, but she reminded herself that he had sacrificed so much to save her and bring her back for their son. She had to be strong for Rhydian, to be the mother he needed. But most importantly for herself. This was her chance to find out who she was without a man, other than her son, in her life. Raesh, Amari, and Roland were all gone. She was free to be herself, whoever that was.

In the evenings, they would sit by the Grand Canal, watching as the city transformed under the setting sun. The water, shimmering with hues of orange and gold, mirrored their fleeting moments of peace. Despite the grief that shadowed their hearts, Kezia found peace in Rhydian's laughter and the beauty of Venice. She knew they would return to the mansion eventually, but for now, this city of canals and dreams offered them a safe haven—a place to heal and remember the love they had shared with Roland. And for them to grow into their own.

# Epilogue

Ten years had passed since Roland had left. Kezia still felt the pain of his absence, but with the love and support of her son, she could move on with her life. She still refused to take lovers, only feeding orally or by touch, something she was not aware she could do until her fight with Luxor. After contacting Alvaro and his mate, she was finally able to master her powers as a succubus with their help. And after meeting Isabella, she finally understood what happened when Roland met with them. The woman was voluptuous and arrestingly beautiful. So much so that Kezia was jealous, but she understood it was the nature of all sex demons. Even Alvaro was tempting.

Rhydian, now an adult, was tirelessly running his father's business, with Luxor and Dorian at his side. He and Dorian had planned to celebrate their love with a handfasting ceremony in the coming days. Lynnox was, of course, beside herself with excitement, and busied herself with the preparations. Kezia was grateful for Lynnox and Luxor's support over the years.

Kezia and Rhydian finished their weekly card game. It was their way of bonding and staying close since he was usually busy with work. The hour had grown late, and Kezia was feeling weary. She made the trek up to bed and got ready for another night in. She sat at her vanity to deal with her mass of unruly curls, fussing with them so much that she once again thought of cutting them. As she closed her eyes and took a deep breath, she felt a familiar presence in the air, as if it were just beyond the veil of her mind. So close, yet so far away.

"You've done well, my love," a familiar voice whispered, gentle and soothing.

Kezia's eyes snapped open, her heart pounding in her chest as she stared at the figure in her mirror. There he was, standing behind her, his form shimmering with an ethereal light. She shook her head, turning in her seat, convinced that it was just a cruel trick of her mind. But then he stepped closer, his hand reaching out to touch her cheek. The warmth of his touch sent a shiver through her body, and she felt the unmistakable truth of his presence.

"Roland?" she breathed, her voice trembling with emotion.

He smiled, his eyes filled with a mixture of sorrow and joy. "It's me, love. I've come home. For good this time."

Tears welled up in her eyes as she reached out to touch him, her hands shaking. As she felt the solidness of his form, her disbelief melted away. "How——" she began, but his gentle kiss silenced her words.

His deepening kiss ignited a passion she had not felt since before he left. He pulled her to her feet and wrapped her tight in his arms, refusing to let her go. When he finally released her, he left her gasping for breath, and the reality of his return settled over her like a warm blanket on a cold winter night. She could see it in his eyes—the pain and longing they had both endured.

"Vala grew tired of my constant sulking," he explained with a wry smile. "She decided I had been punished long enough, and it was time for me to come home to be with my family."

Kezia laughed through her tears, her heart feeling lighter than it had in years. "Thank you, Vala," she whispered to the sky.

Roland chuckled lightly and gave her a soft, but short, kiss on the lips.

"You've missed so much, my love," she murmured.

"I know. And you can tell me all about it in the morning," he replied, his tone suggestive. He picked her up and carried her over to their bed.

Gently, he laid her down, the press of his weight a familiar comfort to her. They spent the evening exploring each other's body, getting reacquainted, and falling in love all over again. She languished in his touch and the fullness she felt when he entered her. Again, she thought she was dreaming, but he reminded her with every orgasm that she was not.

The golden rays of dawn gently seeped into the bedroom, casting a warm glow over the entwined bodies of Roland and Kezia. Her eyes fluttered open, a tender smile spreading across her lips as she took in the sight of him beside her. It was real. He was there with her. Last night's lovemaking still lingered in the air.

Roland's eyes opened to meet hers, and he reached out to brush a stray lock of hair from her face. "Bore da, my love," he whispered, his voice filled with contentment.

"Bore da," she replied softly, leaning into his touch.

They lay there for a few moments, simply enjoying the closeness they had craved for so long.

"We should get up," Kezia said reluctantly, knowing there were many things to address now that he had returned.

"Yes, we should," Roland agreed, though he too seemed reluctant to leave their cocoon of peace.

"Rhydian will be so happy that you're home. He'll be so surprised," she beamed.

Roland smiled mischievously. "I'm sure he knows I'm back. You're still very loud."

She pouted, punching him lightly in the gut. He only laughed more.

With a sigh, they finally rose from bed, getting dressed and preparing for the day ahead. As they made their way downstairs, the familiar sounds of the household greeted them. The passing servants whispered in shock at the sight of Roland, scurrying away to spread the news of his return. Rhydian was in the conference room, his voice carrying through the hall as he discussed business matters with Luxor.

Roland paused just outside the room, taking a deep breath.

Kezia placed a reassuring hand on his arm. "He'll be overjoyed to see you," she said, giving him an encouraging smile.

Roland returned her smile, then pushed the door open and stepped inside. Rhydian, engrossed in a conversation with Luxor, did not notice him at first. But then Luxor's eyes widened, and he fell silent, causing Rhydian to turn around.

"Father?" His voice was barely more than a whisper as he took in the sight of Roland standing before him.

"Yes, son. It's me," Roland said, his voice thick with emotion. "I'm home."

For a moment, there was nothing but stunned silence. Then, with a cry of joy, Rhydian crossed the room in a few strides and enveloped his father in a tight embrace.

Roland held his son close, the years of separation melting away. "I've missed you, too," he chuckled.

Luxor watched the reunion with a smile, giving them a moment of privacy. When they pulled apart, Rhydian's eyes were shining with happiness and relief.

"There's so much to catch you up on," Rhydian said excitedly. "But first, welcome home, father."

Roland smiled. "Thank you, son. It's good to be back."

As they sat down to talk, Kezia stood at the door, a tear of joy slipping down her cheek. Her family was together again.

Lynnox had outdone herself, transforming the grounds of the mansion into a breathtaking scene for the handfasting ceremony. The sun hung high, casting a warm, golden light over the lush gardens where the ceremony would take place. Flowers in every color imaginable adorned the area, and they had arranged a sacred circle of stones in the garden's center. Friends and family gathered, their faces alight with joy and anticipation.

Rhydian stood tall and proud, dressed in ceremonial attire that reflected both his heritage as an incubus and a water elemental demigod. His dragon scales shimmered in the light of the afternoon sun, their iridescent blues reminding Kezia of Roland's. Beside him stood Dorian, his expression a mixture of happiness and reverence. He wore ceremonial attire that reflected his wild wolf nature with earth tones. They had chosen that day to bind their lives together in a celebration of love and unity that honored their shared journey.

Kezia, Roland, Lynnox, and Luxor were present, their hearts full of pride and love for Rhydian and Dorian. Kezia and Lynnox were beside themselves in tears as Roland and Luxor held them close. As the ceremony started, an elder stepped into the circle, holding a length of richly embroidered deep orange linen fabric that featured the heads of a wolf and a dragon with their heads bowed and noses facing each other, forming a heart with a Celtic knot design connecting the bottom of the heart. The artist beautifully crafted it in gold thread, adding more surrounding Celtic designs. At the ends of the fabric were beautiful cords in blue, red, orange, gray, black, and brown.

"Today, we gather to witness and celebrate the union of Rhydian and Dorian," the elder began, his voice resonating with warmth. "Through this handfasting, they pledge their love and commitment to one another, as partners and as family."

Rhydian and Dorian looked deeply into each other's eyes, their hands joined. The elder wrapped the fabric gently around their clasped hands, symbolizing the bind of their lives and intentions. They exchanged their vows with love and heartfelt words.

With their vows exchanged, the elder spoke the last words of the binding. As he removed the fabric, Rhydian and Dorian shared a chaste kiss, sealing their vows with an embrace. The garden erupted in applause and cheers from their loved ones, celebrating the new journey before them.

Kezia wiped a tear from her cheek, feeling a sense of fulfillment and happiness for her son. Roland, sitting beside her, squeezed her hand gently, sharing in her joy.

As the celebrations continued into the night, Rhydian and Dorian danced together under the stars, surrounded by the love and support of their family and friends. The handfasting ceremony at the mansion marked the beginning of a new chapter, one filled with promise, love, and boundless possibilities.

# BONUS CHAPTER

"It's over, Ozzy."

Raesh watched as Roland Ausher picked up the sword. He could feel as Dorjan struggled to move, but was unable to. Raesh thought of helping. He did not want to die like this, but the fight was over. Dorjan had lost. It made no sense to Raesh. Dorjan had the upper hand. Then the sword was suddenly too heavy to hold. Now Roland had it and wielded it with ease.

"I'm sorry," he heard Roland utter.

Dorjan continued to fight against the hold his brother had on their blood, but it was pointless. Raesh could feel his rage, but he knew this was the end. There was no fighting against a water elemental that had mastery over blood control. And was a god, no less. There was a sharp pain in their chest, then the release of their blood—no, his chest and his blood. Dorjan had stolen his love and forced Raesh to give up his body to save his mate. At least Dorjan stayed true to his word and returned Korlue home.

Soon, his body was engulfed in flames. There was the familiar warmth, then nothing. Just the unending darkness, but it was different somehow. There were whispers in the dark this time, and it made Raesh wonder if he was back in the shadow realm. Was this what death—true death—was like? He could not understand the voices, he did not know their language. Was he finally bound for eternal torment? Was he really not going to see Korlue in this life again? Many questions that would go unanswered and an overwhelming sense of dread plagued him. Dorjan had taken Korlue back to club Nirvana. He would be put back to work without him there to protect him. Raesh did not want that life for him, he deserved better. He wanted to give him everything his heart desired and more. He found himself wishing for another chance. That he would give anything to be with his love again.

"If that's how you truly feel, then live, Pak Sang Yong," came a woman's voice.

The sound of his assigned name startled him, making him go ridged.

"Live and atone for your sins by protecting your love." The voice continued, "And remember your promise."

With her last words, the whispering grew to a roar, then quickly became silent.

The halls of the Ausher mansion were far from silent. The echoes of the fierce elemental battle between gods still reverberated outside the mansion's walls. Their clash had left unmistakable marks on the once pristine, now battered and scared, front lawn. Scorch marks marred the earth, turning the grass black and charred. Bloodstained the ground, mingling with the dirt, creating a grisly tableau.

Amidst the chaos, the lifeless husk laid on the lawn, almost overlooked in the aftermath of the conflict. As the hour struck midnight, the husk began to break apart slowly, revealing bits of flesh a little at a time. The moon hung high, its silvery light cast an eerie glow over the husk's inert form. Suddenly, an ethereal aura enveloped it, crackling with supernatural power. His chest heaved with a deep, gasping breath as his eyes shot open, glowing an intense, bright green. Raesh was alive.

The chilly night air bit into his skin as he silently rose from the ground. His unexpected awakening heightened his senses, and he surveyed his surroundings. The sounds of guards and hushed conversations indicated that the mansion's occupants were oblivious to his revival. His movements were fluid and predatory as he silently took down a guard and stole his clothes. They did not fit well, but they would do for now. He slipped past the remaining guards with ease.

The Welsh countryside sprawled out before him, blanketed in darkness and illuminated by the distant twinkle of the stars and the sliver of the moon. Raesh set out on his journey across the Atlantic, guided by his need to get as far away from Roland Ausher and reunite with Korlue.

Upon reaching American soil, he made a stop at his home, where the remaining members of the circus had stayed. Those that stayed behind were up packing their things. They must have heard about Aiden, Sacha, and the others. He was the only one that had returned, and they barely acknowledged him as he passed through to get a change of clothes.

Once properly dressed, he went to Nirvana. The brightly colored lights cast vibrant hues across the urban landscape. The cacophony of honking horns and chatter created a jarring symphony, a stark contrast to the night he had escaped the Ausher house. As he stepped into the club, his presence commanded the room as always, drawing curious glances from patrons.

His eyes scanned the room, landing on Korlue at last. He was in the middle of charming a guest with his impeccable skills. Raesh's eyes narrowed at the guest Korlue was courting as he made his way over to them. The old man got up and scurried away, leaving Korlue confused until he looked up to see why. Korlue's breath caught in his throat and he backed away, his eyes fixed on the man approaching him. Raesh took hold of him in a gentle embrace.

Korlue pushed him back slightly. "Is it really you?" he asked, fighting back tears.

Raesh pulled him tight against him and kissed him with such fire that he thought they would both burn. He left Korlue dazed when he finally released him.

"So, yes," Korlue said, his eyes hooded.

Raesh picked him up and moved to take him out of the building, but a pair of large werewolves blocked his path. He glared at them, growling until they shifted from side to side in discomfort, avoiding his gaze, but still not moving. Before he could push past them, the owner came out.

"Mr. Young! It's so wonderful to see you again!" he said, his voice nervous.

"Move out of my way or I will move you," Raesh growled.

"Yes, well, I can't allow you to just leave with my property."

Raesh narrowed his eyes at him.

"I thought you were dead," Korlue whispered. "I signed a new contract."

"I have returned. Korlue is mine," Raesh affirmed.

"No, no, he is House property again, and I will not allow you—" He let out a blood-curdling scream as he clawed at his face, falling to his knees before toppling over onto the ground.

Raesh had spit in his face, his saliva melting off the skin down to the bone as it spread. The room erupted in screams, and Korlue clung tightly to Raesh as everyone around them panicked. The two guards parted out of the way quickly, and Raesh stepped over the twitching body of the club owner, exiting the building with Korlue in his arms.

In the sanctuary of Raesh's home, he and Korlue made love until the early hours of the morning. While basking in each other's embrace, they talked, recounting their respective ordeals. Raesh still did not know how he survived being run through with a sword capable of killing a god, but he was happy that he did and was back with his love. He remembered watching helplessly as Roland Ausher struck Dorjan down with the blade. Then there was darkness. After a time, he heard whispers in the dark, but he could not make out what they were saying. He felt the gentle touch of a hand on his chest over his heart, followed by a single feminine voice commanding him to live. He remembered feeling warm, as if he was basking in the light of the sun. Then he woke up cold and naked on the ground. He was alive again.

Together, they began the meticulous process of planning their future. They chose a quaint, cozy location in the French Quarter for the bookstore Korlue wanted. They envisioned it as an oasis of calm amidst the city's growing chaos. Their bookstore became their sanctuary, a place filled with shelves brimming with books that inspired wonder, curiosity, and joy. Each book they carefully selected reflected their shared passions and dreams, creating a haven for others just as it became a refuge for them.

Raesh explored his old love of healing through acupuncture. He continued to study until he was ready to help others. He had given up killing for money, but he still practiced his martial arts just in case he needed to protect Korlue and the store. It also helped him work through his lingering feelings of having his body taken from him, losing his circus family because of his perceived cowardice, and dying only to be brought back to life by what he assumed was a goddess. He had made a vow to her to atone for his sins and protect his love.

Their store thrived and became a cherished spot for visitors seeking escape and inspiration. Raesh and Korlue found fulfillment in their new life, their bond growing stronger with each passing day. The bookstore was a symbol of their love and was a new chapter they had begun together.

# GLOSSARY

**Andr** (pronounced: an-der) The solitary warrior, Andr are dragons in human form. They are easily identified by the random patches of black scales with an iridescent green sheen.

**Emori** are a secret order of monks that work for the dragon goddess Vala. They are combat trained and have both human and supernatural beings among them. Their purpose is to keep track of fallen gods and their respective set of Lyr'kin.

**Incubus** is a male sex demon. They cannot reproduce with succubi or other women since they are considered to be among the undead. They are unnaturally attractive and feed off the sexual energies of women they have seduced by coming to them in their dreams.

**Mouras Encantadas** are shapeshifting Galician fairies. They are the souls of young women killed by the fairy king to guard his treasures and the entrance to the fairy underworld. Mouras are not to be trusted, as they are as deadly as they are beautiful.

**Nakaru** are feline familiars. They are intelligent and clever creatures that are both solitary and sociable. Nakaru often work in pairs as caretakers for children of gods. They are like normal cats in how they look, but they are immortal and have a human form and a demonic form.

**Succubus** is a female sex demon. If they are strong enough, succubi will birth triplets as long as they satisfy their sexual energies. They tend to mate with men other than incubi and can drain a man of his life force in an instant, leaving only a husk behind. They are exceedingly dangerous when in heat.

**Umbrae** are living shadows with the ability to detach from their host. They are malevolent creatures that normally do not get along with their host. An Umbra can paralyze and kill via shadows, and light will banish them, but the shadow eating Vanitas can kill them.

# OTHER WORKS BY EMBER DRAKE

# About the Author

Ember Drake is an American author from Columbia, South Carolina. She has been writing since the age of ten and has aspired to be a published author since. Ember has always had a love of dragons and wolves. As a joke, she was told that all she needed was to put them together and then she would be happy. This resulted in the creation of Raesh, who was modeled after her favorite former Power Ranger, Johnny Yong Bosch. Roland/Zaven was modeled after her favorite actor, Matt Ryan.

She had been working on the House of Ausher series since the age of seventeen. It was just three short stories that only included vampires and werewolves, both of which she is a huge fan of. The series evolved from terrible Backstreet Boys fan fiction about three brothers to what it is today.

Visit EmberDrakeAuthor.com for news and updates!

www.ingramcontent.com/pod-product-compliance
Lightning Source LLC
Chambersburg PA
CBHW031341020726
47499CB00005B/1354